D0945293

My Mother's Tears

THE SWISS LIST

MICHEL LAYAZ

My Mother's Tears

TRANSLATED BY TESS LEWIS

LONDON NEW YORK CALCUTTA

swiss arts council

prɔhelvetia

This publication has been supported by a grant
from Pro Helvetia, Swiss Arts Council.

Seagull Books, 2019

First published in French as *Les Larmes de ma mère*
by Michel Layaz

© Editions Zoé, 2003

Published in arrangement with Agence litteraire
Astier-Pécher

First published in English by Seagull Books, 2019

English translation © Tess Lewis, 2019

ISBN   978 0 8574 2 652 9

British Library Cataloguing-in-Publication Data
A catalogue record for this book is available from
the British Library

Typeset by Seagull Books, Calcutta, India
Printed and bound by WordsWorth India, New Delhi, India

*You ought to devise a connection between
the fact that in your moments of greatest truth
you are inevitably what you were in the
past and the fact that only things which are
remembered are true.*

Cesare Pavese, *This Business of Living,
Diary: 1935–1940*

We would have to empty the apartment, of course, and leave the region. A bird flew in through the open window and couldn't get out. Feathers are scattered here and there, on the floor and over the objects. The bird's corpse is here, too. Objects don't fade from your mind as quickly as you think. Sometimes the objects remain frightening. We'll bend down, we'll gather up the feathers, then bury the bird in a forest I love, next to a tree that makes me feel calm, a tree covered in moss that smells of freshly soaped skin, a tree you can climb to breathe in other scents, scents you may not yet know. You say the apartment is an ideal place to talk. You tell me you won't let me take you into my arms until you've heard what I have to say. You add that you couldn't care less if it sounds like extortion. You demand words. It's words you want to believe in.

The Wind-Up Car

My brothers and I had a large collection of small metal cars and none of us felt the need to claim ownership of this or that particular model on the grounds that we had chosen it specially or received it as a gift. The cars were passed on from hand to hand without the slightest hitch. This fine spirit of sharing was put to the test when a model in a class of its own joined our fleet of cars. We each wanted to be the sole owner and driver, even though the notion of a driver suited this car even less than it did the others. Several distinctive features lent this automobile an aura of prestige that occasionally sparked insurrection at the heart of our group. It was much bigger and less true to life than the others with its exceptionally high tires and a disproportionately large steering wheel; it was shinier and, most importantly, it was completely autonomous, in other words, the car had a mechanism underneath that you wound with a key and made the car run on its own for two or three minutes, an enormous length of time, we thought, which ended when the key suddenly stopped turning in the opposite direction to the one that activated, or charged, or fed, the racing car. No epic feat was impossible! The car would, for example, cover the long hallway with stunning speed, crash into the kitchen door, stubbornly try to knock over an armoire, and, to our whoops of encouragement, it would speed off again towards the dining room, repeatedly bumping into chair legs and lamp bases, and find one last open space before coming to a stop wherever its course had led. And so we could begin again, winding up the key and following a new journey in which all surrounding objects became part of the scenery—our apartment was a universe!

Just as it is impossible to predict the path a weighted ball will take when thrown hard, the wind-up car never followed the same path twice, and this pitted us against each other in a competition to be the one who launched it on the most extraordinary, the most insane course, the one we would still be talking about at bedtime. In the spirit of this logic of one-upmanship, in which we shied away from nothing and put the most muddled plans into action, when I saw my mother stretched out on the living-room sofa with her hair like a tragedienne's offering, I had a hunch her head might be an excellent starting point, an unusual pole position that would floor my brothers who worshiped this woman like a prophetess they had to remain on their guard against and whose good graces they could never afford to lose. With the stealth of an assassin, I approached the sofa on all fours and placed the racing car, wound up tight, on my mother's hair. She shot to her feet but could not, despite her quick reaction, untangle the car's key as it dragged her hair, twisted, rolled, and sucked it deep inside the mechanism, leaving us no choice but to wait for the end or for two minutes, that is, for an eternity. My mother didn't try to do anything. Her face wasn't strained or contorted, it was implacable. And her expression, which was the negation of all expression, did not alter until the car's motor finally choked. I can see my mother standing there, the car caught in her hair, glued to her head like a suction cup, my mother going to get a pair of scissors, handing them to me and in a voice more cutting than the sharp object I now hold tight with trembling fingers, in a voice full of contempt that tramples all remorse, in such a voice my mother says: *Cut.* And I see my hand hovering uncertainly above her head; and the unavoidable necessity of having to cut her hair very close to the scalp where the car had worked its massacre, where the white and pink of the scalp is visible; and my mother, who will be left with this bald spot for several weeks, a hole she will never try to cover up, but will instead, displaying her wound, present me alternately as the executioner, the irresponsible one, or the backward child one couldn't possibly scold or truly be angry with.

At the restaurant, for example, you can defend an idea fiercely, with a ferocity borne of your conviction for that particular idea. You come up with phrases that besiege, that conquer, you find formulations that compel, your intelligence brims with spontaneity. But at the end of the meal you founder once you've deployed all your conviction's words and have begun to delight in your good fortune, to feel you've taken on heft—you founder at the precise moment someone sits down at the table next to you, a man or a woman whose mere presence, whose silent, supremely silent presence erases in a single breath the idea you had ferociously defended, the idea you'd considered irrefutable only seconds before.

The Statue

Why didn't my father keep the statue in his bedroom? . . . That way he could have contemplated it
before falling asleep and let it accompany him in his
dreams. I knew the statue was very old, thousands
of years old, and that it came from far away, from
Yemen, a stone statue, almost ten inches tall, half of
its height taken up by the pedestal (the figure had no
legs, or its legs were hidden inside the pedestal), and
the two small breasts set wide apart clearly indicated
it was the bust of a woman, something impossible to
discern from the flat, spare face. My father had the
habit of brushing his hand over the statue before
leaving for work as if it lent him some of its strength
and serenity. He looked at it with such noble tenderness, there wasn't the slightest doubt that it was
the object he was most attached to in the apartment.
I understood his attachment without completely
grasping its depth. More than once, I'd climbed on
a chair the better to feel the statue's form and the

limestone's coarse-grained asperity against my palm. Although the statue was small, to me it seemed colossal, an indomitable mass set on the bureau in the front hall, to which most of our visitors paid no attention. This allowed me to divide all who entered our apartment in two groups: those who noticed the statue and those who did not. I felt a preference for the former and imagined them to be endowed with superior abilities. This tendency to give weight to details has persisted in me and even today I will happily admit that I can't stand anyone who doesn't like cats or who is reluctant to sit on sand or who refuses to go from point A to point B on any path other than the one he is used to . . .

I had been looking for my cup-and-ball for an hour. I'd searched my room from top to bottom, emptying the trunk, digging through the piles of clothes, diving into the wardrobe and under the bed, moving the bookshelf, leaving no shadowy corner unexplored. Nothing! Not a single trace of the toy I also used as a gris-gris or, rather, as a magic wand that would grant me certain wishes if, for example, I managed to catch the perforated ball on the point three, or five, or seven times in a row (according to the magnitude of the wish). Passing the bureau in the front hall, I remembered that my mother sometimes tidied away those of our things, my brothers' and mine, that she considered useless, objects stranded there as in purgatory until she condemned or pardoned them. I opened the last drawer first, the one on top, and then, following some mysterious illogic, the bottom one. When I stood up, I hit my head on the drawer I'd forgotten to close. The impact toppled the statue. I pulled up a chair for a better view: the poor thing's head was smashed. And mine no less than hers! I couldn't lie or hide my mistake, I would have to face my father and hope he'd forgive me, to rely on the depth of his understanding, on his wisdom. I waited in the front hall until he came home, a guard dog snapping at my ankles and preventing me from moving. I despised my clumsiness as much as I did the unholy toy with its power to decapitate. When the front door opened, my father understood at a glance: the bureau, the severed head, my distress, my regret, my dread, he understood it all, but a wave of fury battered his temples, an instinct that can overcome the most gallant of men, inflame him, inject him with the brutality of a pirate, of a torturer, a violence that will not dissipate without some astonishing act, a cry, a resonant gesture. His face calm but with his jaws clenched as if he wanted to grind his teeth to dust, my father slapped me.

Sitting quietly on my bed, I stroked my burning cheeks, relieved the moment had passed, feeling no hatred for my father and completely convinced of the blow's necessity, of the coming reconciliation.

My pain and distress would not last.

I only had to close my eyes to be reborn.

Rustling cloth can have the impact of an explosion! In a grey dress, my mother loomed in the doorway, as imposing and impassive as the figures on Assyrian bas-reliefs. Her body refused to come closer, would not cross the threshold of the room, but her voice reached me, resounding from another era. Victorious, Victorian, it pierced me to the marrow, shook me, lifted me, penetrated and shrivelled me. In a tone of frivolous hatred that disdains and condemns the surrounding domesticity, her voice said: *Go, go and see what you've done! Go see what a state you've left your father in! Do you hear me? . . . Go look at your father!* He was sitting on the worn red-upholstered chair my mother deemed dreadful, but because it had accompanied her husband since his adolescence, she'd ended up tolerating it as one tolerates an inalienable defect—like angular bones, a birthmark, a drooping mouth, short fingers, bad eyesight. Seated on his chair, my father was leaning forward, trembling. He hid his wretched face. When he sensed me near him, he pulled away his hands, I saw the face of a man in tears, a face that revealed what he would look like in twenty years with wrinkles around his eyes and deepening furrows, with the irreversible exhaustion that spreads over every patch of skin, withers it, dulls it, eats away at it, but I also saw that he was imprisoned in the chair, as if enveloped in a metallic shell with close-set bars and padlocked door, my father was trapped in this cage like an animal subjected to various experiments and that may one day be freed once the analyses were completed if the head of the laboratory allowed. My father couldn't bear the fact that he had hit me. He was repentant. He hoped his tears would absolve him, would dilute his despair. Just as I was about to tell him how little it mattered, how much I loved him, just as I was about to nestle into his arms, to smell the scent of his skin, that same triumphant voice full of belligerent glee suddenly returned, that voice come to quicken our sorrow and complete my father's humiliation: *Now that you've seen . . . Go! Disappear!* And the grey of my mother's dress gleamed with indomitable radiance.

What can you expect of a man who goes into raptures at the sight of fruit pulp, or bowing sunflowers, or the flight of a dragonfly, or a shade of nail polish? . . . What can you expect of a man who is satisfied with burr marigolds, the smell of hyacinths, a man who searches for the words to describe not only these things but their gradual decay as well? . . . You take each of my fingers in turn and pull on them until they crack. You push them backwards. You bite the tips and smile, perhaps with love.

The Fishing Rod

When I was ten years old, I was given a fishing rod. A real fishing rod! With nylon line, a reel, and a black-and-gold handle. A gift from people I didn't know, a client of my father's, accompanied by her husband. As soon as they arrived, this woman and this man—both very tall and very good-looking—handed me the fishing rod. I didn't dare touch it, doubtful the gift was meant for me, doubtful that people I was seeing for the very first time could behave like Santa Claus or, better, since Santa doesn't have the same captivating superiority, doesn't move with such grace. He wouldn't provoke either the same fear or the same attraction that grew in me and, instead of making me any bolder, tormented me and gave me—despite my efforts not to look ridiculous—a confused, vacuous air. I stood stock-still and looked at the couple with stirrings of panic. Why on earth were they offering a child they didn't even know an object as charged with dreams and adventures as the fishing rod they were now holding out to me with insistent grace, an object I didn't dare take in my hands for fear it might disappear between the floorboards, or slip through the gap in a broken tile or fly off, mocking my stupidity and torpor? . . . Accepting a gift can resemble combat or capturing a castle. *But it's for you . . . The fishing rod's for you . . . Go on! Take it . . .* My father enunciated each word as if he were speaking to someone who was hard of hearing. My father was irritated to see me so timid, so hesitant, my shoulders hunched in a sign of exile, so devoid of courage, treating words and my own body like enemies or allies ready to betray me, and if no one else heard it, I knew my father's voice was also saying other, less pleasant things, phrases slipped to me on the sly, phrases he didn't need to articulate for me to hear them. I tried to gather my wits as best I could, to find some coherence, something reassuring, like an algebraic formula or an irrefutable proof. I was searching for rational explanations when all I had to do was look up and extend my hand without further ado. There was nothing more to it: a magic couple had appeared in our house with a fishing rod in their baggage and the rod was not meant for my two brothers. How could I drop my false impassivity? . . . How could I overcome the impossibility of being born someone else? . . .

The woman had run her fingers through my hair, fingers as silken as my mother's scarves, fingers that left me quivering from head to toe, fingers that spread so wide they could enfold my entire head and this woman had directed a curious smile at my mother, that is, her smile had nothing unusual about it at the start, but as soon as it took shape, as soon as it reached its apogee, instead of remaining in place for two or three seconds as is a smile's wont, this smile turned into something else, perhaps in the way her upper teeth pressed down her lower lip, into a smiled reproach, perhaps, yes . . . , that's exactly it, a smile with a hint of rebuke that may have forced my mother, who never lowered her eyes, to look away. But what did such looks matter to me! . . . I now had a fishing rod in my hands. Like a star. A bag of pearls. I was its new master. Nothing else mattered. They could all forget me. They could take up their conversations—about art, world conflicts, social injustice, poverty, the economy, good restaurants, coming vacations—I owned a fishing rod. No one could claim the contrary and no one could take it away from me. How could a bicycle, a pair of skates, a kite, a sword, a model racetrack compare? . . . There are objects that await us, that suit us well. Maybe we don't know, we can't imagine, and without this couple I could have lived in total ignorance of this fishing rod and the pleasures it would bring. On the first night, I slept with it in my bed. I woke to look at it, to touch it, to make sure I hadn't dreamt it, to make sure that this sorcerer couple had indeed come to our home, that the woman's hand had stroked my head, that the gift was real. If I had died that night, I would have wanted to be buried with the fishing rod, to have it accompany me to the place where uncertainties are banished, where destinies are resolved.

The next day, at dawn, I was allowed to go to the river. To go by myself. And until I turned thirteen, I would go to the riverbank with my rod, hooks, little lures, bucket, a pack of butter cookies, and a litre of raspberry lemonade that tasted like cough syrup and foamed at the slightest bump. I also had a pair of yellow rubber boots, much too large for me, that my mother had consented to buy and thanks to them I was able—although it was forbidden—to wade across the river in the shallowest spot. To get to the river, I had to take the bus that passed behind our building, get off at the first stop, and continue on foot for about twenty minutes. I sat in the front of the bus near the driver, proud of my fishing rod, my boots, of being able to go to the river alone, and occasionally, sheltered from all mishaps, I watched my reflection in one of the bus' rear-view mirrors. Then I would try out different poses, different expressions. I made different faces until I found one I decided was the perfect fisherman's bearing. People smiled at me.

Bus drivers have a machine in their hands and they know where they're going. A peculiar noise, a smell, a flickering light, a passing disturbance, a throb of menace, they observe everything and take note. They're able to avoid the worst because they have no choice. They are at once in the crosshairs and on the lookout. Bus drivers push buttons and the doors open, directions are followed, passengers get on or off, roads are taken, the dispersal of passengers decreases. As for me, I had my fishing rod and I knew where I was going. Passing the driver, I let drop: *Goodbye, sir, thank you for your careful driving. I'm going fishing.* All discord evaporated. Dark masses dissolved into dust. I was heir to a joy safe from chaos and the void.

The very first time I settled myself on the riverbank on a round rock under which a few weeds grew that tickled my calves, as soon as I cast my line with a worm stuck on the hook, I knew. I knew that no fish would ever come nibble on my line. If it were any other way, I'd have given up the bus ride, the bucket, the lemonade with the light pink foam that stained my lips, and the fishing rod. At home, at first, they laughed at me and made fun of my efforts. They nicknamed me the *fish-hobo*. But they soon grew tired of my empty buckets and my failures, which I continued to experience as ineffable successes.

You want to know why I don't have any mirrors in my own apartment, which is probably a third of the size of this one. You climb on to a chair. You're ready to inundate me with theories about homes without mirror. You're prepared to quote books that allow no uncertainty . . . I see your lips taking offence. I see your eyebrows growing infuriated . . . You want me to buy a mirror.

The Merry-Go-Round

At the neighbourhood pool where we liked to gather and which the surrounding buildings gave room to breathe, our activities were divided between games in the pool—diving into the water and underwater, cannonballs, naval battles, water polo—and games on the ground—running races, hide-and-seek, going down the slide, gymnastics. Yet the main attraction was the merry-go-round, whose shape evoked certain torture devices that once adorned fortified castles. Constructed from a circular wooden platform raised a few centimetres off the ground with a metal axle through its centre on which was mounted an iron structure we pushed against to make the platform spin, the merry-go-round held six people—the legal number of riders—but that rarely discouraged the pushy latecomers, whom I liked to join. As the merry-go-round gained speed, some faces became flushed, others turned pale or began to break down, but most often we were happy to spin slowly. This gave the more daring boys a chance to hold a girl on their laps, a boldness I sometimes ventured, but for me, boldness was only relative since Romaine, a green-eyed blonde who ruffled my heart, never ended up on my lap. I preferred not to know the joy she would give me in accepting my invitation because I didn't want to face the sadness I'd sink into if she turned me down. Romaine sat on the other boys' laps and other girls sat on mine. And so the merry-go-round spun with no real danger.

Now and then we had a speed contest. Who could stand the fastest spinning? . . . Who would be King of the Merry-Go-Round? . . . There were usually two groups of four to six boys (the girls may have had their reasons for encouraging this kind of foolishness, but not for the world would they have wanted to join in). The selection within each team followed the same procedure: we spun the merry-go-round faster and faster until one of the contenders, his eyes shut tight, grimaced and begged for mercy. In short order, each side had only one contender left. The two survivors faced off in a final round that inspired cries of enthusiasm and admiration, or jeering and insults depending on which side was shouting. What honed the desire to win was the victor's prize: for ten seconds, he could kiss whichever girl he chose from among the spectators. Romaine, who watched this jousting with good grace, would always take a bar of chocolate out of her green purse during the final round and suck it languorously, lost in sweet reverie, her eyes fixed on the last two rivals' efforts. The chocolate melted between her lips, darkened them, and to clean them Romaine had a way of licking her lips I found infinitely alluring . . .

Several times, I was proclaimed King of the Merry-Go-Round! I could have kissed Romaine—I was dying to—but there again, out of a pride that was no more than shyness, I always headed towards other girls. My excessive desire made me inflexible. In the end, I considered my behaviour cowardly, shabby, unworthy of the King of the Merry-Go-Round, and I promised myself one morning that on my next victory, come what may, I would approach Romaine and prove my preference with a fervent kiss. There was a tournament two days later. Romaine was one of the spectators. I was able to make the last round without much effort. Only the final, fatal confrontation remained. No one knew my rival, a stranger to the neighbourhood, a Greek boy whose family was passing through our town. Short and chubby, with a cheerful face and no neck, he was immediately drawn to our contest and wanted to join in. The Greek boy was anything but impressive. Still, how did he make it to the final round? He must have used all his resistance to make it that far or maybe the others, sensing my determination, didn't have the guts to face me. How wrong I was! The Greek didn't steal his victory. He was there because no one could match him. Clutching the metal frame with his plump hands, he kept pumping the merry-go-round faster and faster, as if being on the spinning rocket didn't cause him the slightest fear or discomfort. His cheerful expression never faltered. It was enough to make you sick. The merry-go-round might spin faster than it ever had before, faster than it ever would again, the Greek—I sensed it more than saw it—was as relaxed as if he were on the deck of a cruise ship, delight sculpted in his rather soft flesh. With such an adversary, kissing Romaine would remain a fantasy, especially since my ears were ringing and I had no strength left to pump the merry-go-round. I only wanted it to stop. The dishonour of defeat awaited me. I had to act! To do something, anything! Casanova, in the story of his life, is careful to distinguish between honest ruse and deceit. I don't know if I was a simple cheat or an honest trickster, but when I realized I would never beat the Greek, I sidled up to him so I could deliver him a Homeric—

that is, epic—kick in the shin, with no holds barred, a kick loaded with all my love for Romaine, my disgust with this spinning torture, and my irritation in the face of that impervious smile, come from so far away to thwart my plans. It worked better than expected, this forced destiny brought the immediate surrender of the Greek, who, try as he might to convince everyone with his protests as he clutched his leg, no one understood his babbling. I was declared the new King of the Merry-Go-Round. A tottering king! A feeble-looking king! My legs were stiff, my heart in a whirl. Two black sidewalls limited my field of vision and gradually narrowed it. Without a thought, driven by a will that someone one else was directing inside me, I went up to Romaine, kissed her—certainly less than ten seconds—and immediately felt the urgent need to disappear with as much dignity as possible before my status as King of the Merry-Go-Round began to fray and earned me some sarcastic comments. All I had to orient myself was a five-centimetre wide strip of light, dazzling as lightning, thanks to which I was able to reach the changing rooms, then the toilet. As for Romaine's kiss, so eagerly awaited and so chocolaty, I had to relieve myself of it over a toilet bowl that smelt of chlorine and pee.

I forgot a few round slices of carrots on the bottom of a pan and they've turned into small black stinking piles. In the bottom of this pan, which I've obstinately scrubbed, determined to save it whatever the cost, armed with several rags and a maniacal patience, in the bottom of this pan, now dull, scratched, and scored, completely lustreless, I can finally bear to look at myself, I can bear the uncertain spectre of my face that appears and wavers.

My Mother's Tears

When I was born, my mother burst into tears. On the photograph taken of the two of us a few minutes after my birth, you can clearly see—despite the lipstick freshly applied to her lips, despite the foundation spread over her cheeks—you can clearly see her moist eyes. My mother in tears. After a crying fit. My mother's tears. A tearful birth. I don't remember who said *terrible flood* while looking at the photograph. My mother had slipped a few things into the pocket of her silk nightgown and as soon as the child arrived, in other words, as soon as I was there, even before she looked at me, not yet knowing if she had brought a beautiful baby into the world, a healthy baby, with no defects, with no infirmities, my mother had apparently plunged her hand into the pocket of her nightgown and pulled out a cosmetic case. She put on fresh lipstick. She dabbed foundation on her cheeks with no concern for what had just left her womb, relieved to have less weight to carry around along the street, up the staircase, when getting up in the morning and going to bed at night, those three and a half kilos of male-child flesh from which she would never completely free herself despite the nurseries and nannies, despite her travelling and her weeks abroad, despite my father and my father's patience. The crying fit, I'm told, occurred just then, immediately after my mother had applied her makeup the first time, made herself up for nothing because it smudged, staining her honour, giving her for a moment a mad woman's face, a body with stiffening limbs, exhausting themselves in spasms as if ropes were pulling them in all directions, drawing them apart, assailing her furious flesh. In another era, a century earlier, there would have been a gleeful rush to photograph my mother, who would have then adorned the plates used to illustrate the woolly theories shrinks invented at the time, images that inevitably evoke a sense of disquiet through the inmates' troubling beauty, their groans and frantic breathing, their shuddering limbs. When her makeup ran, it would have revealed the pallor of my mother's cheeks, the cheeks of a strong, shrewd woman who in these circumstances was obtuse, unable to free herself from an obsession she'd already tried to wash away with a flood of tears, an obsession that, to be sure, should have a heavier, more cunning weight than the child in her womb, defeated by mere contractions. In maternity wards where mothers endure extreme violence before collapsing with joy, just as you might hear their screams, my mother's crying fit was no doubt punctuated with invective launched in caustic tones like impossible, impermissible detonations. It couldn't have lasted much more than two minutes. No one dared comment when my mother put on her make-up for a second time, especially not the doctor who had known this woman since he assisted her first two deliveries, this woman next to whom other women's beauty was laughable, this woman whose eyes could blaze with funereal ferocity and dissuade all attempts at reverence or conciliation.

Just as my mother had ordered, my father was waiting in a room devoid of flowers because she hated seeing those death throes in vases and found their odour as viscerally repulsive as the smell of carrion. He was to wait until she joined him there. The male head nurse, who spouted mundane wisdom like clockwork, imagined it would be a good idea to tell my mother that my father's presence would be a solace to her and he offered to go get him. This nice boy suddenly discovered how the cunning, malice, spite and extraordinary superiority of beings—of whose existence he was previously unaware—can set fire to phrases, transform them into burning lashes that smite the skin and inscribe incurable wounds that will keep him from ever opening his mouth again without first considering whom he's dealing with, whom he's talking to, or from thinking that any woman is the same as the one who preceded her or the one who follows.

The photograph was not put in the family album.

There were photographs of all kinds in our albums, just not this one.

I was seven years old. The photograph slipped out of an envelope where it had been put with old postcards. Someone picked it up and said *terrible flood*. I can't say if it was a man's or a woman's voice. The voice was of neither sex, neither high nor low, neither slow nor rushed, a voice escaped from a phantom body that only said *terrible flood* without putting any feeling into those two words, confident they contained an incontestable truth, an objective voice with a tone someone might have when giving testimony about an accident observed from his balcony, answering with complete confidence at the time of police interrogation. This *terrible flood* terrified with the force of its truth. The speaker offered no objection or, more likely, didn't dare object when my mother snatched the photograph away and, with a smile striking for its calm violence, said: *No need for silliness*. And the conversation continued as if nothing—not the sexless voice, my mother's 'No need for silliness' or the legitimate questions about the photograph, dropped from who knows where— had happened, as if my mother's voice, her cleverness, her charm always managed to prevent a pall of silence falling after those moments of unpleasantness that waken multiple curiosities or hone existing ones and so stifle those moments as quickly as possible. Words blanket other words, scatter them, erase them. My mother's words had the power to charm, to placate, that is, to banish unwelcome opinions, to confine them to a cage, a prison. I had ears only for the sound of her steps retreating from the room. I separated out the impurities: the laughter, the arguments, the pleasantries, the true stories; all I heard was the cupboard door open, the lid of the dustbin rise then fall, the cupboard door close, and my mother's steps going in the opposite direction, my mother heading back towards us after having got rid of the image that might encourage someone—not anyone close to us or anyone reasonable—but might inadvertently encourage some naïf, some idiot to ask, to wonder why, to want to clear up the mystery behind this *terrible flood*.

She will return, her hands empty. When I open my eyes and look at her, her hands will be empty and there won't be the slightest evidence of what she has just done. For a second time she will condemn me, cast me out, she will condemn the instigator of the terrible flood, the wisp of a son, disposable, the little man-child unworthy of attention, to whom this condemnation will never be explained. My mother has rejoined her guests. She banters, she buzzes from one person to the next, my mother who harvests smiles from the adults as well as the children; my mother who, for others, wears a glowing mask radiant with sunlight, whose dazzling lips pearl her words with sublime sensuality, imbuing them with flesh and life. She illumines and is crowned for it. None can match her beauty.

I waited for her eyes to fall on me, I waited for her to utter words for me, for me alone, an intimate, reassuring phrase to soften the tragedy, to assuage my fear, but my mother—queen bee reigning over her subjects—didn't spare me a glance, she dismissed me, banished me from her hive, as she had the photograph, non-existent, discarded, in the darkness of the dustbin with the cigarette butts and paper towels, with the coffee grounds and empty cartons, with the crumbs and vegetable peels.

If you knew how many masks I wear to please you. If you recognized all my false smiles, all my false words. If you were aware of it all, you'd be alarmed and you'd leave me. I dine with your friends. I tell them stories that make them smile. I don't disappear. I conceal myself. They tell each other it was a perfect evening. Me, I tell myself nothing. To please you, I put on clothes that aren't mine. A bully's clothes. An aesthete's get-up. A boxer's kit. I don't have a bully's arrogance, or an aesthete's condescension, or a boxer's strength. I can only wear their garb. Just to make you happy.

The Swing

Was it because part of the cliff had collapsed? Or did
someone decide to install it here? I don't know. Who-
ever had the idea of setting up this swing on the
beach must be dead by now: the metal stanchions
were already covered with rust back then, as were
the chains. The red paint was still visible in places,
but the wood of the seat had darkened. As soon as
I'd stripped off my clothes and pulled on my bathing
suit, I would start to swing with all my might, to rise
as high as possible, feet aimed at the sky, legs
stretched straight out to pierce it, to reach the highest
heights, to brush it, caress it, but the dome of the sky
kept retreating, evading my toes, the sky billowed
like the cape of an impassive giant and slipped away;
the sky that could have carried off the beach, the cliff,
the sea, the immensity of it all. This morning pleasure
never disappointed me. Afterwards, my body glisten-
ing with sweat, my heart light and bursting with life,
I picked up my cap and remained sitting on the

swing that hurt my bottom, that imprinted itself on my buttocks. I sat there for hours, delighted with my fate, able to look into the greatest distances, surprised by the pleasure that filled me, beyond desire, without words: in other words, nothing passed through me, not the slightest sound, not a single idea, only a soothing void. But for this to happen, I had to be seated there, on that swing. Nowhere else could I have found or regained this state of abandon, of ignorance, completely devoid of expectations, no expectation even of the moment when my mother would call in her refined voice—like the call of a rare, a precious bird, a voice you would instead expect to hear during intermission at the opera when, among a group of people discussing the production with intelligence and passion, a voice rises, perhaps a touch too shrill, too loud, and delivers the decisive remark, so fine a gem that the remaining conversation seems mere costume jewellery. This was the voice in which my mother spoke when she handed each of us two sandwiches she'd prepared that morning, sandwiches we'd chosen during breakfast, if you can call 'choosing' the act of repeating exactly the same ingredients we'd listed the day before and which we would just as certainly list the following day since at that age repetition and familiarity give so much pleasure. Five years in a row, we'd taken ten-day holidays on a beach in southern Italy, ten days spent almost exclusively on that beach, the beach with the swing, which became our beach and never attracted much of a crowd since I have no memory of ever having had to share the swing with other children.

Behind us was the cliff face. I saw it as a challenge. I wished the swing had been placed on top of the cliff, set up on the edge of the void, the feet of the stanchions cemented into the earth to stabilize it, so that no storm or ill-intentioned soul could move it. I would have liked to hear a voice pronounce self-evidently, as if it were inconceivable that no one had thought of it earlier—*let's move the swing to the top of the cliff*—and I'd have liked for this crazy suggestion not to have the slightest hint of madness but exactly the opposite, to seem utterly reasonable and wise. What sensations of fear and delight came from alternately flying over the earth and the void, from hearing the creak of the chains drop into the emptiness then sound again, what a sense of anxiety these creaks would spawn from the fear of a possible break, how the vertigo of rusty squeaking would blow over my soul, bringing a hint of nausea! With each swing came the herald of death, then death, then it would all begin again: the thrill, the horror and the grip of fear. Together, my father, my brothers and I could have carried the swing up to the top of the cliff. But no voice sounded. No one would ever utter the magic words and the swing would stay where it was, in its place, for ever.

If I ever went into the water, I rarely stayed long, only long enough for a few strokes of my arms, a single kick. Mostly I went in, the better to return to the swing, to smell that smell of flesh, water, iron and sun, oblivious of time passing, gripped by the odour that enchanted my surroundings: in other words, I could have worshipped a grain of sand for what it was and that would have been enough for me. My brothers loved swimming, yelling, playing ball, climbing on each other's shoulders, inventing contests and rules, puffing out their chests, choking on bouts of uncontrollable laughter that were carried to us by gusts of wind. Stretched out on a mat, my mother read books of philosophy. Seated on a towel, my father perused specialized journals that untangled world conflicts and even here, safe from worries, from the telephone, from his clients' questions, nothing softened the two furrows that rose at an angle from the inner ends of his eyebrows and met about three centimetres above them such that the lower half of my father's forehead was permanently marked with a triangle. This lent him an air of such deep concern that even when he was daydreaming, we believed him prey to profound thoughts. As for me, I was happy with the swing and my arcs.

The ten days were like an eternity in which I lacked nothing and nothing got in my way. My brain was stripped bare and I revelled in its nudity. Naked on the beach, in the arcs of the swing, I lived this parallel time with no threats, no abysses, no possible falls. Except for the moment of our final departure, which demanded of me absolute control to keep from crying, that is, to keep from collapsing into sobs, from falling under a spell, from harming my mind with a possibly irreversible madness—my brothers, on the other hand, had nothing to hide, their games would continue in different forms, for them nothing was ending, nothing dying—aside, then, from this rupture when a mere word could wound me, I see only one blot on this lucid canvas, on these five times ten days spent in southern Italy that filled me with a soothing image of calm and brought me gorgeous folds of incomparable joy. It's late afternoon. Not far from the swing there's a little boy, smaller than my brothers, smaller than I. He has a blue bucket and a few plastic toys and he's building a tower of wet sand. Where did he come from? He's there for the first time. He's alone but isn't afraid.

He's busy. He constructs his tower. He decorates it using a twig that allows him not only to add windows, doors, fluting and arrow-slits but also friezes and arabesques, all of which he creates with delicacy and delight. He occasionally breathes in puffs of wind which stretch the skin of his chest and reveal the ridges of his rib cage. When he turns to face me, I approve his decorations with a smile. I suggest a few more and we communicate through our gestures of silent children. There is no rivalry between us. We don't ask each other any questions. Our whole purpose is reduced to being nothing more than two creatures who are there and expect nothing from each other. And that suits us perfectly. We're pleased with this state of affairs. Soon, my two brothers show up. They look at the little boy, they say hello, they smile at him, they lower their heads to their chests and look at the tower, which sparkles, then they look at me. With enormous grace and power, they launch a kick at the tower of sand and gold. An implacable kick. A devastating kick. My brothers laugh and run towards the water. And I join my laughter to theirs. I laugh on the waves of my brothers' laughter as the narrow-chested boy gets up and leaves. Without looking back. His blue pail over his shoulder. With his gait of a very young child. Hesitant. Tottering.

You say it's worth taking an interest in cultivating cacti, in raising rabbits, in the veins of leaves and in sperm whales' blowing, that it's worth studying writers and composers, climbing mountains, stretching out on the sand, collecting amulets, that it's worth taking the trouble to understand the mechanism in a watch, or to play cowboys and Indians. You say it's worth talking to you and devoting myself to words. Then you add that only the stingy keep silent and withdraw.

The Square Room

She would not let us come in. It was her room. Her chamber. A square room filled with books, a single red-leather armchair, and a very long, low table on which stood a Chinese bowl and a black vase with a bouquet of artificial orchids that my mother perfumed several times a week with an atomizer. My father only ever entered the square room if my mother was in it and after he had asked permission. For the most part, he didn't go in at all. As for us, my mother would have killed us if we'd dared set foot in the room. My two brothers never mentioned the square room, they ignored it, they'd forgotten about it, and did not spare it a glance or word. I couldn't tell if their behaviour was due to indifference or some kind of wisdom. As for me, when I passed the square room, I couldn't help but slow down. Even if I had decided to speed up or to break into a run as soon as I got near the door, I slowed my steps, at the mercy of some gravitational force or some hand placed on my chest holding me back, obstructing my path, even forcing me to make a detour around the other side of our apartment to reach my bedroom.

Out of carelessness or malice, my mother sometimes left the door to her temple ajar and I often saw her sitting in the armchair, legs stretched out in front of her or tucked beneath her, reading, always reading, as if what she held in her hands had the power to tear her away from the world, as if a book could seize my mother and carry her off to a world created just for her, a world closed to me, one I admired and envied, a world that had the advantage, for my mother, of erasing time, the city, the telephone, the praise or insults of mere mortals. Through the crack in the door I could watch her for twenty or twenty-five minutes without her noticing my presence, which both delighted me (I saw my mother without her seeing me) and distressed me (it gave me the measure of my inability to arouse her interest, to compete with the higher presences in whose honour my mother had built a sanctuary, inaccessible to inferior beings and the uninitiated, a place for her alone that only my glances caressing her flesh could darken). I was fascinated by the movement of her eyes over the pages, their brisk back and forth, their nervous motion that came close to hypnotizing me, and the words, moved by some mysterious power, came alive, took shape, abandoned the lines of print, left the book and entered my mother's eyes, crossed them, filled them, flowed in her blood, the words kept her alive like sap, nourished her, sustained her furious beauty and the smiles I tried to decipher, the words reinforced her intelligence or at least one aspect of it, the most visible, the least tender, the one that confounded, chastised, that demeaned with ease. I became certain of only one thing: without words, my mother would pine away, would be dead to the world. I thought of the two canisters of petrol on the garage shelves, I thought of the many matchboxes my father bought from the street vendor, printed with pictures of our country's regional folk costumes. Would I dare let my soul swell with savagery and set a book on fire and toss it into the library? . . . Would I dare lash out, launch an assault against the ecstatic melodies that followed one after the other inside the square room? . . .

As soon as my mother noticed me through the crack in the door, her gaze would fix on me intently, but suddenly, as when a rapidly spinning top bumps into an obstacle that kills its dance, the intensity evaporated and her gaze signalled the vaguely parasitical element I embodied for her. I would flee as fast as I could.

On a train journey, for example. I can speak about a topic that interests you, one that is important to you, a topic that could keep you awake your entire life. And I speak about this topic relentlessly, lucidly, because I have faith in my perceptions. My perceptions are not derived from anyone else. It's a strength—not an intelligence. And so you listen to me. But here's something you did not expect: the words tangle in my mouth, my body trembles, my nose bleeds, my bones clatter and the world exasperates me. I sputter, my lips move pointlessly, my teeth chatter and finally silence falls, ailing, repugnant, silence spreads over us like a body on an operating table, abandons itself to the hands of strangers. And this happens very quickly, over the course of a few seconds. Then comes the fear of speaking again, for several days the fear of being unable to complete a sentence, fear that a word could finish me off, fear of saying even the simplest things, like asking for a book of stamps at the post office or a kilo of artichokes at the market. And then, there's living with this fear.

The Carving Knife

How can I forget the abruptness with which my voice, overnight, suffered the most extreme distortions, rising, falling, breaking on a sentence or on a single word, plunging into low registers, rapidly rebounding into high notes, and all without warning, without time for me to adjust or formulate a tactic, as if it had to take its prey by surprise, squeeze its throat before it could make the slightest protective move, draw up a defensive plan, or find a perch from which to confront the black holes and loss of balance? These sonorous aberrations escaped me and made mockery of my efforts to stabilize the timbre of my voice, to prevent being reduced to silence, to keep from having to express my emotions only with smiles or mimicry and from being forced to admit that our infinite array of sensations was now restricted to two categories as grotesque as 'good' and 'not good'.

In the classroom, my voice's whims elicited some laughter, some ridicule, especially from the girls who usually giggled and guffawed but were so profoundly indignant, they must have felt it only just to castigate the one who'd had the bad taste to render ridiculous the transformations that assail the flesh in early adolescence when he should have affirmed those valiant, heroic changes, as one of our classmates had understood so well. This was the classmate who, after gym class, when it was time for the obligatory shower enforced by our teacher, a former army captain for whom hygiene and respect for rules were part of an inviolable code that no argument from a student, that is, from an inferior being, hierarchically subject to obeisance, could have altered. This classmate, then, delighted by the obligatory shower, by the rule itself and its inflexible application, puffed out his chest and straightened his shoulders. He strutted up and down the locker room so that everyone could, once again, take note of the impressive black bush that flourished above his genitals, the dark thicket that taunted us, kept us at bay, threw us back on our fate as insufficient beings, as toddlers and glabrous scoundrels. I would have paid any price to be endowed with a fraction of his aplomb and rascally panache, this classmate who was not merely a gorilla and who, ever since he had discovered the value of the privative '*a*' amused himself by calling us not *bêtes à poil* (naked beasts) but *bêtes a-poil* (hairless beasts).

And we found this homonym very clever.

Evenings, when my family gathered at table to eat the well-balanced dinners my mother prepared for us, were the time when this transformation proved most painful, not so much because of the smiles my family refused to stifle as soon as my voice betrayed me like a coin dropping or a cable popping—smiles I joined in with good will—but because of the unpredictable moment when my mother, suddenly serious again, her upper lip faintly twitching, her nostrils flaring less than usual (also faintly twitching), would turn to my father and declare in a voice that brooked no appeal, a voice that corners its prey, that administers ill like the blow of a bat, my mother would command: *Do something, dear, to make the boy keep quiet!*

And I kept quiet.

Crushed with shame and loathing, my eyes fixed on the blade of my knife, I kept quiet, yet for the first time screaming mute cries of rage and vengeance all the while. The screams in my head abated and gradually disappeared as the blade expanded, filled all available space, cleared away my suffering. In the cone of silence that surrounded me, I heard only a sleek incision, irresistible, infallible. I could feel the ease, the obedience with which the knife blade plunged into the meat and I longed to be that knife, that blade. I wanted to be as cutting, as brilliant, as able to wound, to butcher, slash, assassinate. I wanted to rise from the table and soar, shielded from my family's eyes, and the moment my mother, lips parted, would pronounce her condemnation, I would first slip between her inviolable lips, between her gnashing teeth, then I would pry her upper jaw away from the lower and, at the very moment she was ready to cry out (for help or to dissuade me), in one blow, like a prestidigitator, I would slice off her beautiful pink tongue and let it drop onto her plate, wriggling like a fish out of water at first, but soon inert, its colour fading, its arrogance seeping away, curling up like a scrap of boiled meat that assumes a cadaver's fixed shade of grey and is thrown peremptorily to the dogs.

I'm not dying! I can write letters of complaint or of recommendation. I can use all my powers to defend a book or a person. I can advise, comfort, laugh, make cutting remarks. I can take sides with fury or intelligence. I can fulfil my professional obligations and complete household chores. I can leaf through travel-agency catalogues without disgust. I can even book two plane tickets for a *Dream Weekend of Adventure in the Floating City*.

The Darts

He would wrap the darts in a small bag and slip
them into his pocket. We didn't have a dartboard at
home. We only had these two darts: the red one and
the green one. Every two or three weeks for almost
two years, my father and I would take off without
my brothers or my mother. We would leave the city
and head north for one of the many forests in the
region. My father's announcements of these sylvan
escapes would fill me with joy even though, as we
closed the door to the apartment, a weight settled on
my shoulders like the spectre of a guilty conscience
trying to soften my resolve but I was able to shake it
off by racing down the stairs to reach the lobby,
breathless, seconds before the lift. This allowed me
to play the bellboy and hold the door for my father,
deferentially holding out my hand into which he
never failed to place a coin. From the moment he sat
behind the wheel, my father would smile for the
entire drive as if this road to the forest, whatever the

weather or season, had the virtue (despite the orders of various medical specialists he grudgingly consulted now and again) of consoling him, of easing all weariness and woe, of scattering all tedium, banality and adversity. We always drove to the same spot and parked the car under a somewhat solitary beech tree that hung over the road. My father led the way and I delighted in his unreasonable behaviour and wisdom in banishing the political crises and stock indices in which he had once or twice tried, without much conviction, to interest me.

As soon as we entered the forest, sheltered from suffocating principles and precepts that stun, we behaved like two mad men, two monkeys, two rebels against decency. We kicked at the trees' bark, we tore up the moss and stacked it into piles, we tossed leaves over our heads, we ran, sang, blew into hollow branches, opened our mouths to devour everything around us and drew loops on the ground with our feet. We invented dangers, enemies, battles, various monsters to be vanquished and others to be saved (even without knowing much about them, I could tell the difference between harpies, unicorns, phoenixes, griffons, sphinxes and other worrisome hybrids). We invoked the spirits of the forest, we offered them our joy, we roared until the veins in our temples bulged and forced us to stop and calm down a bit, to recover some serenity. Sitting on a log, we listened to the sounds of the place. We let them approach us and bewitch us, but not completely and not for long. Before any mysteries could upset us, before any anxiety set in, my father took the two darts out of the bag, waved them before my eyes, let me choose between the red and the green and, with a word or a glance, designated the first target to hit. We had the agility of freebooters, the luck of high-stakes gamblers. Our darts were implanted in pinecones, in tree trunks, stumps, in a root, a knot, a fork. Most often they hit the mark we'd assigned them.

And so we advanced, from one target to the next, from exploits to points lost, from sighs to points won, until we arrived at a small farmstead on a plot bordered with a larch tree at each corner, a house covered with shingles on three sides that must have once served as an inn because a sign from an earlier era showed a schematically drawn bed and blankets. We rarely encountered other guests and if we did— which happened no more than three times—they soon disappeared, at least for the duration of our visit. As a rule, the two women who lived there— Floriane and Régine—were alone. They welcomed us with open arms, hugging us like family, like intimate friends they'd been longing to see. They brought us drinks and fruits in season: plums, redcurrants, bilberries, apricots, cherries, apples, pears, and occasionally even a few wild strawberries, which I crushed between my lips one by one, delaying the moment of swallowing them, happy to hold on my palate what I would not have hesitated to declare—seduced by hyperbole as children that age often are—the very best flavour in the world.

I loved these two women with their soft pallor, their broad hips, their fine, fitted blouses. I liked to listen to their voices, free of pretension, when they told me stories about animals or spoke colourfully of the flowers and plants they grew. If the two women looked very much alike (the same slender hands, the same generous mouth, the same gait, the same brief fluttering of eyelids), for me it was in their breasts that they were most sisters and once I'd quenched my thirst, I was impatient for only one thing, for my father to disappear with one or the other of these two women, so that I could stretch out on the bench, my head resting in Floriane or Régine's lap, my eyes half-closed, lingering at the gates of sleep, her breasts hovering over me, breasts I contemplated like sublime flesh I didn't have to share with anyone else. And what can I say about those many exalted moments when, reaching for some object or other on the table, Floriane or Régine bent forward, her bosom brushing my cheek, her breasts spreading an exquisite asphyxiation over my face? All this —the intermediate moment, the sight of the breasts above me, the touch of them, the stories they told— instilled in me a beatific calm that held only the pleasure of being alive and the desire for the moment to last. The sound of my father's voice as he descended the stairs brought me back to reality. A reality become more tender, more desirable. Floriane and Régine would kiss us before we left. We played no games and spoke no words on our walk back to the car. I did not look my father nor he at me. We merely held each other's hand, our warm, our panting, our knowing hands.

So many words we would have to do without. We hear them here or there, we come across them written just about anywhere, in newspapers now outdated, on posters that are only attractive when torn. Horror and obscenity, perched on mountaintops where they rule without regard, have recently begun to fill you with fear and indignation.

The Orchids

Because of an ache that was tying my stomach in knots, I had left school in the middle of the afternoon, overcome with worry and the smell of my body dripping with sweat. Ever since a classmate had been operated on and the surgeon had removed from his stomach a ball of hair, a tooth and the beginning of an ear, I was convinced, when I rubbed my hand over my own belly, palpating and pinching it, that I could feel, not organic elements but bits of metal (screws, rings, watchbands, coins, nuts and bolts) rusting in my intestines, piercing them and turning them yellow, infecting them in the worst possible ways, leading me to death by poisoning, which might still be prevented through evisceration—a word I'd learnt when in Rome, thanks to my father's connections, we saw Orazio Borgianni's painting of the martyrdom of Saint Erasmus. Leaving school, I became certain that I would have to undergo the same suffering if I wanted to be saved. I saw Saint

Erasmus, lying on his back with his stomach slit open and his arms along his sides; I saw the three torturers busy winding his intestines around a winch, metres of blood-streaked viscera that contrasted with the pallor of his corpse even though he was still alive, even though his mouth implored, his darkened hands extended as if to stave off the pain, to bear it, perhaps conquer it. What was killing him would keep me alive. My discomfiture, as imaginary as it was visceral, would not last long: twenty minutes walking in broad daylight under the watchful eyes of the starlings pecking at the sky was enough to dispel it without harm.

The apartment should have been empty.

I had just walked in and, caressing the Yemeni statue with my index finger, I heard moaning, little sobs that aroused as much as curiosity as concern. Without any rhythm, the voice would get carried away, then fall silent for a few seconds, would rise or fade away gently, intensify, grow quiet, rebound in spurts. This voice that I guessed belonged to my mother communicated delight as well as distress, disgust as well as pleasure. I approached the source of the sound like an unknown area, a terrain full of traps over which one must proceed lightly, with graceful evasions, with the suppleness of an acrobat. The door to the square room was not closed. To clear up the mystery, I only had to nudge it open. With the tips of my fingers, disregarding the rules and threats that unsettled us and made us subject to a commanding force, I pushed the door.

My mother was curled up on the low table, one hand bunching her skirt up to her thighs, another pressed against her sex, as if glued, suctioned, impossible to remove, my mother coiled, writhed, pressed her legs together, her one hand still inseparable from her sex, as the fingers of her other hand, spread wide, pressed the flesh of her breasts, crept down to her stomach, returned to her chest, and all this (one hand fixed and one moving, her body convulsing) elicited groans in variable tempers, from ecstasy to anxiety, from oppressiveness to wonder. For this body, for my mother, I felt an attraction I suppressed and I suffered at not being able to savour this show performed for no one. Several dozen books surrounded her, some open, some closed, some standing upright and, scattered here and there, like dark bursts of purple against the white of the covers, were artificial orchids.

Drawing up a list of your possessions can bring a measure of reassurance. If my mental faculties were stable, I could draw up an inventory of my belongings. I'd learn what I'm missing. I'd like to have binoculars instead of eyes. I would see every detail of your face. Without your knowing, I'd see its most subtle inflections and would experience the world's inflections. With that, it might be easier to breathe.

My Mother's Tears

Why throw away the only photograph that shows us together, her and me? . . . There aren't any others. I've looked through all the albums, photograph after photograph—the *terrible flood* is the only one of just the two of us. She wouldn't have done it lightly. She must have wanted the photograph to disappear. How can I sleep with that thought? . . . I have closed my eyes and pictured the moment when my mother, her foot on the lever that opens the lid of the dustbin, threw away the photograph, the photograph of her with me, my mother crying into this refuse hole, my mother and me, tossed into the bin the next day, then loaded into the dustcart and poured onto the scrap-yard, my mother and me mixed in with tons of rubbish that clings to us, carries us off, tears us apart and then nothing else: fire, destruction, ashes, oblivion. I had to deflect this fate. Barefoot, trembling, fearing the creaking of the floorboards or the whistling of the windows, I moved through the living room like a believer summoned by his god. I wished all sounds would stick to me, not spread at all. I wanted to stifle every noise, crush each one against my skin. I wanted to lose all substance, to shrink, to be reduced to a shadow, a silhouette. My body invisible, chest flattened, terrorized by the objects that take possession of the night and give it weight, objects that live and bewitch, I remained immobile in the centre of the room, hoping that a star would explode, that the house would fly away, that my mother would appear, barefoot like me, bosom heaving beneath her nightgown, a trace of saliva in the corner of her mouth, breathing heavily, her nostrils flaring nervously, my mother, who would have suddenly remembered having done something foolish, a distraction that had to be set right immediately, even in the middle of the night, so that sleep and good health could return, so that no discord would tear at her soul, would drag her over furrows that make one ugly. My mother rushes to the dustbin, opens the lid, kneels, confronts the dull stench, rummages through the evening's scraps and finally retrieves the photograph, which she pinches between her lacquered nails. She smiles because she has broken the evil spell. She notices me in a corner of the living room. She forgets to ask what I'm doing here at this hour. She wraps me in her arms, holds me tight. Her voice says: *Look*!

I almost lost our photograph. And she'll kiss my cheeks, my mouth, my ears, my neck, my eyelids, she will kiss me with her loving lips, kisses that perfume the body, wipe away all fears, so that I feel like I'm stretched out on the edge of a forest, feeling only the breath of the wind on the leaves and my mother's breath scattering all mistakes and misunderstandings. An infinite silence . . . Nothing moved in the middle of the room. There was only the heaviness of objects in the night. I crossed the room in a single bound. When I opened the dustbin, instead of the bag full of filth, there was another. No matter how many times I stuck my hand in and felt around on all sides, I found nothing. I held my fingers under my nose and smelt only the sharp, solvent smell of clean bin bags.

You claim you know me. So tell me why, even though there are no omens, even though nothing is weighing on us and we are happy to be here, tell me why, when a conversation is beginning, I suddenly think of so many good reasons to wish it would end? . . . Why, when I glimpse someone shaking out a white sheet through the window, I see it as a sign of surrender? . . . And tell me why ringing bells are signs of joy and lightness for some and warnings of attack and death knell for others? . . .

The Diving Board

One, three, five or ten metres—we could choose the height according to the level of our courage and our desires. No one was trying to establish superiority. My brothers never tired of climbing up to the highest boards, performing audacious or incongruous moves. Every time they took a run and picked up momentum to fling themselves into the air, I quivered with admiration and vicariously shared their vigorous joy. Watching them, I got the idea of bringing along a notepad and pencil to draw them executing the dives that pleased me most. I deconstructed their movements to best represent, one by one, the different stages of each jump. When they discovered my drawings, my brothers felt flattered. Thanks to these sketches, they saw more clearly what to change to improve their dives or to come up with more subtle moves. We introduced a new gesture, for example, a turn of the hand or the head, elements I wrote down so we could discuss them later and invent the perfect dive. Never before had we formed such a homogeneous and unified team, free of any outside influence, with the dive to be perfected in our only universe. We were close to the goal. There was only one shadowy zone: how to place an arm in the small of the back. My brothers always positioned their arms badly and questioned the move's usefulness. My drawings were no longer any help. For me, this positioning was the key to the balance, the ultimate gesture that would ratify our success. We had to get it right, whatever the cost!

Since I saw that my brothers were beginning to neglect what they were starting to consider a caprice of mine, I resolved to climb on to the diving board, not to perform the dive myself—I wouldn't have been able to—but to show them the harmonious lightness of the arm's placement as I wanted it.

Caught at the far end of the board, I immediately regretted this initiative that allowed for no retreat without pitiful failure. I concentrated on my *mission*. I even jumped defiantly on the board. I flew into the air, perhaps I placed my arm in exactly the right way, but I landed in the water not head-first, but on my bottom with my legs stretched straight out in front of me, pulling off a variation of what we call, with sarcasm and disdain, a *belly flop*. It's the noisiest, most brutal and most painful way to enter the water. Climbing out of the pool, I hardly heard my brothers' laughter or the voice of the lifeguard asking me how I was. The water in my ears muffled all sound. I felt a searing pain in my lower abdomen as if my testicles had flipped and entered into me, an agonizing sensation that required me to withdraw into the one place that was peaceful although stained with an unpleasant memory: the toilet.

Conjectures flashed through my brain, flowing, mingling, disappearing, leaving lots of room for the worst and flooding back. I could already see the blood. Mangled flesh. The horror, compacted into the crotch of my swim suit, viscous and swarming. When I reached the toilets, I first stood in a petrified stupor, then, eyes closed as if I were pulling the bandage off a pustulant sore, I peeled off my suit. I had to open my eyes. Face it. The sight was unlike the one I'd imagined: my two testicles formed a single ball whose skin, a translucent pink, was stretched tight. Trembling, I looked at this ball, as ugly as the vocal sacs that swell when frogs croak, but here the skin was so thin, a twig could have punctured this water lily bud. I waited silently for the catastrophe, which could come in one of two forms: either the testicle would burst like a balloon or it would deflate like an inner tube. In the first case, the pain would be intense but brief, in the second less intense but drawn out. I didn't dare sit down. I didn't dare move. I remained standing, legs slightly apart, eyes rigid from the approaching disaster. The consequences of this jump into the water assailed me: sterility, limpness, chastity, shame, forced asceticism, flight into the desert, misery, bitterness. To escape this dire fate there was only death, that is, suicide. I pictured it for the first time, I ran through all my reading for stories of voluntary deaths I could imitate. These reflections kept me occupied long enough for me to have to admit that the state of the swelling hadn't changed. And if the sensation of pain persisted, the pain itself seemed to be lessening.

Somehow or other I made it home. I shut myself up in my room and dared to fall asleep. Gloomy amphibian songs and visions of slit veins accompanied my slide into sleep. Waking, I felt a bit better, my body somewhat calmer. I had to lower my pyjamas. Take another look. Face it all again! I promised myself, if rest had cured my ill, that I would never again try to convince anyone at all against his wishes. And ever since this perfect 'flop', despite all urges and desires, I have kept my promise!

In the spring, a poet I like sees three roses. The first three. And these three roses wake his ardour. He leaves everything behind to follow spring as it arrives. A poet is capable of this. It's nothing to boast about. No reason to claim honour. Today, a century later, spring has arrived. And I think of this poet. And I think of leaving. But I don't go.

The Hand

My father wasn't very interested in art, or only indi-
rectly, because his work required it or because some
obligation made it necessary. If he read a book now
and then, it was a work of history (never a novel or a
collection of poetry) and for several weeks we would
see it lying around on a chair or the coffee table, its
title printed in very visible letters as if to remind the
reader of the importance, grandeur or grandiloquence
of the subject it treated, such as *The Life of Catherine
de Medici* or *The Final Days of Alexander the Great*
or *Mme de Maintenon's Influence on Louis XIV* or
The Esotericism of Philip II or even *The Glory of
Tamerlane*, thick books with illustrations on their
covers that inspired me to invent stories that were no
less far-fetched than the real ones I knew nothing
about. The knowledge of history my father acquired,
even painted in broad brush strokes, was not at all a
pretence or a social pose. Famous men and women

truly interested him and if he'd had the time and the talent, he would have liked to be a modern-day Plutarch.

My father never went to art exhibitions (what works we owned had all been bought by my mother). He rarely went to concerts—he would fall asleep after ten minutes—and even more rarely would he go to the theatre (even if that hadn't always been the case and even if he occasionally went with us). He did not have a problem with the theatre per se, but with actors. My father had for them a level of mistrust, even disgust, which would have made him a keen critic, quick to see the effects or counter-effects each actor deploys or avoids to win the audience's affection and admiration. If he were a despot and able to disdain life as much as the powerful do, my father would have reinstituted a potter's field for actors.

Late one afternoon, my father returned home with a cumbersome object that he set down in the middle of the living room, calling us to come. The rare eccentricities he indulged in delighted his three sons and embarrassed my mother, who bore a charitable smile in these circumstances because she knew the annoyance would be short-lived and she could return everything to its proper places as soon as our backs were turned. In an engaging voice, my father said: *A fantastic thing! I bought it in an art gallery . . .*

He smiled with generosity.

I thought of how nice it was to see my father like this, far removed from the worries and troubles that make up the essential part of adult life: obligations, savings, the children's future, fear of the unknown, unfounded accusations, hope for honours, family equilibrium, expectation of congratulations, illusions kept silent, all those small deceits for which we take the bit between our teeth even though the world deserves that we talk about them, debate them, even though nothing is simple, nothing natural, unless you achieve the rare state of contemplation that, even though it has nothing to do with it, resembles the slick stupidity into which so many men and women sink. And all the possible transgressions, always classic and conforming, won't change anything!

The crate my father brought home looked like a kind of pedestal made of two materials: iron for the lower half, Plexiglas for the more important upper half. We were puzzled: the pedestal was filled with sand up to the edge of the metal part. My father, excited by his purchase and the surprise he had in store for us, held his finger for several moments to a button no one had noticed. A steady mechanical noise had set in. We saw the sand tremble and shift. We saw tremors form circles, then something emerged from the sand very slowly. We tried hard to identify it until we recognized a closed hand, a fist, and this very realistic hand began to rise and as it rose, its fingers unfolded and spread. The hand rotated, confidently at first in search of an object to grab or another hand to clasp, and at the very moment we had the feeling the hand could seize the object or the invisible other, the hand, confronted with emptiness, stiffened, as if frozen for the time of the painful revelation, then it sagged and began to sink, returning to its position as clenched fist, before disappearing beneath the sand. We were enthralled! Such an object would make sleep impossible! My father was delighted with our reaction and re-engaged the mechanism. Only my mother remained silent. I couldn't tell just how appalling she found this work, how unsophisticated she once again judged my father's taste, but what I did realize was that she refused—in the name of culture, of her exquisite taste, of her extremely refined sensibility—to understand the disquieting fascination and voluptuousness this hand, doomed to failure, inspired in us.

You tug on my lower lip and pinch it without smiling. You say: *As soon as I let go, you will confide a thing you dislike, a manner you can't tolerate, something I don't know yet.* You tug, you pinch, you hurt me until I agree. But at least I can choose when . . .

The Tall Candlestick

Always wearing a faded, baggy sweatshirt, jeans that squeezed his waist, and gleaming sneakers with the logo of the most sought-after brand, Uncle Paul looked like a prematurely aged adolescent or an adult who had forgotten to adapt his wardrobe, which, in my father's eyes (inspired by a quote from some writer or other) was a double affront: first to the adult world and second to the world of adolescents. My mother, usually filled with disdain for bad taste in clothing, never said a word against Uncle Paul. In truth, Uncle Paul was no relation at all, but since he often stopped by the house and was close to the family, we got into the habit of calling him that, especially since most of our real uncles lived abroad which limited and complicated our family reunions. Uncle Paul usually stopped in to see us on his way home from the dental prosthesis laboratory where he worked as a technician. On every single visit, this fake uncle brought his fake nephews fruit candies to our delight, even if he handed us the box without a word or the slightest expression, like a kind of obole he had to pay in order to be admitted into an apartment he liked. Our negotiations for dividing up the fruit candies involved veritable strategies aimed at reaping a maximum of our preferred flavours. Chance (a throw of the dice, the short straw or an *eeny–meeny–miny–moe*) designated which of us would be the first to choose the first candy, then, taking turns, we emptied the box of its thirty-three marvels, hiding our preferences, which varied from one day to the next, mine generally tending to yellow or burgundy, that is to say, lemon or blackcurrant.

Uncle Paul had one vice according to my father or one virtue according to my mother: he wrote scripts. We didn't have slightest idea what was in them until a young director decided to stage one of Uncle Paul's plays. My excitement at the prospect of going to the theatre was as intense as the boredom I suffered during the performance. Still, I wanted to be interested, I forced myself, I tried to control my feelings, but in vain. I was ignorant of the fabulous ingredients that create the best stage productions, the front that makes everything seem easy, as if all the power were released by a simple snap of the fingers. I have forgotten every detail of Uncle Paul's play. I only know that I escaped boredom by prolonging certain words, words I straddled to ride off to Régine and Floriane, towards their breasts against which I would crush myself with delight and languor, sheltered from pretence and vindictiveness. The young director knew a few journalists and several articles in the local press presented Uncle Paul as one of the best dramatists of the moment. My mother had cut out the three articles that came to this consensus and she spread them out on the table in the living room where we'd gathered religiously to hear her read them aloud. When she was finished, my father, exasperated by the rigmarole, shrugged and left the room without comment, while my brothers and I wanted most of all to look at the pictures of Uncle Paul. I was ready to believe I'd been mistaken, that this ageless, potbellied man was the genius the papers claimed he was, but I could not explain away the fact that he never had anything to tell us. A story now and then or a pleasantly delivered anecdote would have been enough to win me over as one of Uncle Paul's most faithful allies.

Two days after the final performance, Uncle Paul came to the apartment with his usual grave expression. And yet, from the way he swivelled his head in short jerks, it was clear he had trouble hiding his sense of success. My mother congratulated him, piled on comment after comment that sparked his delight. She spoke so well of the play that, listening to her, I had the impression she was talking about a different one, much shadier, more tragic and more exciting. Whatever our reasons, we can turn to gold the dusty words of those we love and admire! Deafened by glory and bursting with vanity, Uncle Paul made a misstep: he asked my father, misanthrope for the occasion, for his opinion. My mother sensed the possible disaster and answered for him, recalled her husband's lack of taste for the arts, his ignorance of literature, she lamented his lack of sensitivity, his imbecility, but Uncle Paul insisted. What he wanted were unfiltered words, straight from my father's mouth. Words of complete candour. Because his opinion was being asked with such persistence, my father replied in a slightly strained voice that he had never heard anything as repellent or as false, that the ability to move others was not granted to everyone, that writing for the theatre required superior abilities of which Uncle Paul was completely devoid. He even spoke of verbal rubbish and first-rate popular claptrap. He followed this by advising our uncle Paul to dedicate himself to developing dental prostheses, to good workmanship and similar improvements. Finally, my father concluded his speech with these words, which were also sincere: *You are a friend of mine and I like you without theatricality*. Uncle Paul froze in his rigidity, if that is even possible, into a kind of three-part column: legs, torso, head, the whole impenetrable, like ruins that had never moved despite two thousand years of rain, sun, tremors and gusting winds. Only his index finger vibrated—but with what speed and tension!—his nail scraped at the paint on the tall red candlestick, paint he managed to scratch away, leaving a hole at least a centimetre deep. Rage, fury, resentment and a taste for murder and vengeance were all concentrated in this index finger that excavated madly until the body-column rose, that is, until imaginary archaeologists activated the winches placed beneath Uncle Paul's arms and legs to raise him, set him upright and lead him towards the front door.

After a month with no news from Uncle Paul, since my brothers were worried, my mother announced that Paul had been so hurt he never wanted to set foot in our home again. My father, never emotional over the loss of a friend, retorted that an artist's susceptibility is directly proportional to his lack of talent. He then turned to his three sons to warn them that they would have to come to terms with the loss of fruit candy . . .

Uncle Paul is still alive. Father of three children, he has a respectable paunch. He talks to his children gravely. He lives in a large apartment and runs a laboratory that manufactures dental prostheses. He worries about spending his money which he has invested in very safe stocks. He is without passion, without excess, without faith. He has assured me that he lives in complete harmony with himself and his family. He has no memory of the large candlestick.

I like to take your head in my hands. I like to feel your skull between my fingers. I feel it, roll it, press it, I know its shape, its orifices, its bumps, I run my hands over every inch, I enfold, I embrace it. I grip your world in my two hands. At night, I like to fall asleep with this bone under my arm.

The Green Pumps

My mother looked at me sweetly and I abandoned myself to the kindness in her eyes. I was alone with her in the bedroom. First, she sat me down on the chair facing her vanity table and its three mirrors. She rested her hands on my shoulders, not heavily, with a pressure that crushes, but with a soothing, elevating one. My mother was saying in a delicate, incontestable voice: *You're not to move. Just let me do this. Listen to your mother. You don't want to make your mother angry now, do you?* . . . And once again, there was sweetness in her look that could have made me apprehensive, like animals wary of affection used to trick them.

I was five or six years old. My mother was combing my hair. She was proud of how shiny, blonde and fine it was. She wound my hair around her fingers, breathed in its smell, took strands in her mouth, immersed herself in my hair, which was long enough for her to plait and tie with a ribbon. And right away, she gave me a kiss on my temple as if to thank me, to comfort me. After that, she put lipstick on my lips, a little powder on my face, blue eyeshadow on my eyes, mascara on my lashes. Her smile didn't waver—a smile that banished all anguish and sorrow, that assuaged all worries and sadness, a smile that bewitched this son, all too pleased to disappear into his mother's sighs and beating heart. Again, she gave me a kiss. Then she said in the same delicate, incontestable voice: *Look what I bought for you.* She went to the armoire and took out a package. My mother, so very sweet. Sweeter than ever. I didn't understand. In the package there was a green dress with very fine embroidery in darker green on the cuffs. She helped me undress. She hummed to herself. Songs I didn't recognize. She was still smiling, of course, but I would have been unable to detect the few lines of worry—if, in fact, they even existed— that must have shadowed her lips. My mother lifted me onto her lap. She caressed my arms, the back of my neck. Her glances were intimate. She said: *You're my little princess. No one knows, but you're my little princess.* She opened one of the vanity drawers and took out a pair of green pumps. She brushed her hand over the pumps and explained that they had been hers, that she'd kept them since she was a little girl, that I could put them on whenever I was in the bedroom with her. And my mother's eyes sparkled; my mother's voice so passionate. She took me by the hand and spun me in a circle around her, she pressed me to her belly, she smiled with joy at my airs and graces, she repeated that I was her little princess and all I could see was the frenzy of her delight, I plunged into the labyrinth with her. I was the source of her pleasure, I didn't inhibit her in any way.

What path does suspicion follow? . . . How does it erupt so suddenly? . . . Fear rose without warning. I understood that her response wasn't meant for me. Her caresses grew suffocating, her caresses carried death in them. I needed air. To leave the room. I freed myself from my mother's arms and ran out. From the doorway, I threw the green pumps at the vanity and its three mirrors. They were never mentioned again.

My elbows are propped on the table, my nose and mouth hidden behind my hands, both thumbs under my chin and my index fingers pushing on the corner of each eye. The pressure is light at first, more of a caress, as when you're brushing away a lash. No need for disproportionate measures: a few strokes back and forth of a fingertip are enough. But the skin at the corner of my eye swells, hardens, enough for this minute transformation to annoy me. I press once more on the same spot, but with more strength, more conviction, and the more I press, the more the skin swells, like a small bead that insists on growing. I quickly summon all the strength I can bring to my fingertips, concentrated right there, with maximum density, and I crush the two bumps of inflamed skin that start to itch, to burn my eyes, the entire surface of my eyes, from one corner to the other, one shore to the next. I scratch, I press my fingers into my eyes, I scratch some more. My eyes are mush but I don't stop, caught between unbearable pain and a pleasure prolonged only by not ending this carnal shudder, this gasping massacre. Mystery and panic of the eye. You say: Stop gouging out your eyes.

My Mother's Tears

My father had surely put the bag with the photograph out on the kerb. Three flights of stairs to go down. Three landings wavering under the neon lights. I clung to the handrail in the staircase, I fought against each step, each step was an enemy to fend off, to stab, and in the excessively white light, in the malignant coolness, days passed like a great void that swallows one's existence. How old would I be when I reached the street? . . . How would my face have changed? . . . Three floors would be enough to make me an old man, to fill me with a dying soul. I pressed the tips of my fingers against my temples until the commotion inside weakened. The sorcerers have no power. There's no such thing as people who cast spells. Their conjuring tricks dispel each other, blow each other away, expire between two claps of the hands. A child can, without a guide or a protective hand, ward off the steps of staircase that haunt him. I descended, my fingers soon confidently holding the iron railing, filled with a boldness they'd finally recovered.

Outside, the light from the lamp post reassured me with its pink hue. I was no longer in such a rush. I wished the light could fall into my pocket so I could take it back to my room and keep it under my pillow, near at hand, ready whenever I needed it.

Bin bags were piled high on the pavement, but I recognized mine, ours, with its green string dangling, perhaps out of coquetry, against the black. I untied the knot and took hold of the slightly wrinkled photograph, whitewashed with several drops of milk. Thank goodness! It was intact. My mother hadn't ripped it up and the drops of milk left no trace. I looked at the picture in the soothing light and felt my flesh warm. From the end of the street, a voice with accents of eternity reached me. It spread out, suffused my heart and disappeared down the other end of the street, simple words that had turned into a melody. Isn't this how men—without wanting confidence and in the gaps between words they scatter haphazardly—offer the best part of themselves? . . . My return to bed was easily accomplished. All night long, I held the photograph tight against my stomach. Why did that voice of neither sex say *terrible flood*? What contagion did it presume to find me guilty of? I repeated the accursed expression to myself. As if my mother's tears represented a danger, as if my mother were about to be lost, about to drown in a terrible tide that inundates, that washes away, far out to sea, that engulfs distant lands forbidden to small boys who are afraid of losing their mothers, boys who have to brave the night and their fears to overcome the affliction, to face down the cataclysms that weigh on their mothers' hearts. I crushed the seeds of worry, I reduced them to dust I could hold in the palm of my hand and blow out of the open window. Farewell, *terrible flood*! . . . Farewell thoughts that cause dismay! Births bring mothers incomparable joy. Children arrive on earth, they are born for this purpose. For this first and foremost. For mothers' joy to erupt. A joy without uncertainty—complete. And mothers' tears are there to celebrate this joy without pretence. And for that alone.

I take a dozen books from the shelf and in their place, I rest my head, upright, my nose pressed against the back of the bookcase. I breathe in the smell of wood and books. I remain like this until I hear nothing but the batting of my eyelids. Sometimes a consciousness approaches from the left and reads all the books to my left with prodigious speed, a second or two for each book, not a single sentence can resist, and this consciousness comes closer to my head, pierces it, penetrates it, records my feelings, my past, my ideas, it seizes everything, takes it all away. It leaves my head and starts reading the books to my right, leaving me there in a pallid void, a gentle stupor.

The Picture in the Room

I knew the picture by heart. If anyone had asked me to draw it, I could have closed my eyes and my heart would have guided my hand. I wouldn't have had to think twice. If my attention got caught up in the picture, lingering on the hourglass, for example, or on the candle stub, on the dangling scarf, on the shape of the trees, on the canopy bed or, as happened most often, on the rather brutish figure of the angel, with his clumsy hand, his blonde curls that stood out so clearly against his blue-black wings, if my attention was caught by God the Father on His cloud, His hands extended before Him like a diver, or even on the Virgin Mary kneeling and facing me, the Virgin discomfited by the angel's news, if my thoughts wallowed in the colour of the floor, brown spattered with orange, all this was nothing compared to the figure in the painting that beguiled and captivated me: that of the cat. My mother, her voice shriller than usual, in a tone that chiselled her words, massacred them, my mother would say: *That cat represents the devil . . . That's why it's so frightened and leaps up on hearing news of the Son of God's arrival on earth. You see? . . . That cat is the devil.*

That's not what I saw at all. Besides, the books and scholarly studies my mother had surely read carefully made no difference to me. For me, the cat in the picture was not the devil. It looked like a cat in our neighbourhood: the same small ears, the same thin tail, the same yellow eyes that looked at you and contained lives of which you knew nothing. I had named him Titus. We had long conversations together. It is incorrect to think animals can develop personalities—they have personalities.

Whenever I was alone, I would let Titus into the apartment. He would immediately sit on a kitchen chair, right across from me, his head erect, his ears perked up and, as if imitating me, he would place his two front paws on the table exactly the way I rested my hands on the table. Once we were installed this way and only in this way, face to face, could our debates begin, and while it's true that I spoke a lot, I did appreciate Titus' comments, especially when, with just a few meows, he begged me to reconsider what I believed to be the case, to observe those around me more closely, to not let myself be swayed by hurt or worry, to be more disdainful of my brothers' advantages, not to mourn anything, to turn my indignation into pronouncements, to avoid asking useless questions. Titus knew how to receive my comments and thoughts better than a diary.

One afternoon, my brothers surprised us in the middle of an animated conversation. They didn't miss the chance to laugh at the little brother who had no friends other than a cat. In their desire to consolidate their privileged place, they recounted the event—employing all of their dramatic talents—to my mother who laughed at her older sons' clowning and excesses and sighed over the raptures of her third son who was content to amuse himself with a cat's purring like a wastrel with a dewdrop. I don't believe my mother forbade me from letting Titus into the apartment, but I was afraid my brothers would interrupt and taunt us, not suspecting a much greater danger awaited us. With three of his acolytes, my older brother managed to catch Titus. Then, following a predetermined scenario—like the one we had seen on TV—the heroic band climbed to the top of the staircase and my brother, the chief bandit, the one holding Titus out with his arm extended straight, my brother, who thought himself clever in grimacing like a tyrant, let Titus fall into the void. I wanted to fight them. I wanted to tell them I loved Titus, and that killing him would be killing me! But what can you do against three or four boys who are tougher than you? What can you do when your intelligence is eking out drop by drop and the words that might have stopped the massacre refuse to hatch and remain caught in your throat? If I could have found the words, I would have stopped it all. A few syllables from someone with oratorical skill and blood is tamed, hearts calmed, battles end, pride is deflated, base behaviour censured. More than computer science, history, geography, algebra, literature, geometry or the sciences, that's what should be taught: How to put your finger on the sentence that will lead things where you want them. How to change the world with a word! Alter its trajectory. Turn it upside down! But that time, I was frozen by the fury sealed inside me. The words could not get out, they burst confusedly inside my head. In the film we'd seen, when the cat landed on the ground, it quickly regained consciousness, walked a few metres, its insides dragging, its flesh bloodied, rolled its head in its paws and collapsed, stone dead, under the eyes, shining with delight, of boys at whom evil had begun to gnaw; boys who, one day, howling the credos of financiers, prophets or generals, would know how to destroy, break, rape, flay and torture all citizens of the same violence eternally deployed as soon as the leader's signal resounds. In my brother's scenario, things took a different turn. Once he hit the ground, Titus didn't move. Not a shiver. Not a spasm. He was killed on impact. Excited by their adventure, my brother's gang reached the bottom of the staircase, where I already stood, filled not with sadness, or hate, or the desire for vengeance but with a disgust that swirled in a closed circuit through my throat, my chest and my stomach, a liquid bitterness that corrodes the best souls. After my brother flipped the cat over with the tip of his shoe like a piece of rubbish, like a bit filth, as he leant over Titus for a better look at the face of a freshly dead cat, my brother suffered the unthinkable, an unhoped-for assault by Titus who, in one movement, reared up, leapt at right at my brother and dug his claws into his face. Titus clung to it, hung there, had no difficulty finding the meat of his retaliation. My brother screamed bloody murder, his skin glowed. He pulled at the animal, shook his head, spun in circles, tried to throw off the bristling monster, the enraged devil. None of the boys dared come close, sensing things would end badly, that interfering would only make things worse, that their role was reduced to nothing, to watching, listening and not forgetting. The prodigious animal's caterwauling drowned out my brother's cries of pain and fear and he now stood stock-still. The cat alone would decide when to let go. That privilege was his. One of Titus' claws was especially pernicious, tearing open my brother's cheek from the top of his left cheekbone to the corner of his mouth. Despite the stitches, despite the ointments applied for months to the scar, it was clear it would never disappear. I can still see Titus' icy expression during the attack, his body extended, his fur on end. I see my brother's bloodied head, his lacerated skin. I hear his convulsive breathing, his useless tears, the wet stain on his trousers spreading, his face collapsing. Deeming his vengeance complete, Titus released his victim. He walked off about twenty metres towards the shade of a tree in the courtyard and gently slumped to the ground. My brother, on his knees, submissive, kept his eyes wide open. They were filled with emptiness, with a void that possessed him. By the time I got to the tree, Titus had disappeared, disappeared for ever ... In the picture pinned to the wall of my room, the cat looked like Titus.

While a bus driver careens like a madman over bumpy roads, while new landscapes flash past, while encounters could be taking place and discussions had, while life, as unbearable, exhausting, elusive, absurd and terrifying as it is, passes by, the sight of someone close to me asleep at such a moment, sleeping an animal sleep, exposing his baseness —mouth agape, cheek pressed flat, neck flushed, Adam's apple twitching—is a sight that disgusts me. Although this slumbering person's lot may seem enviable, I personally lack the cowardice necessary for the feat of sleeping in any circumstances. What is more demeaning than this abandon without true fatigue, without voluptuousness, this defection from being? . . .

The Black Comb

All March and April, the rain seemed to never want to stop. My father, who worked at home more and more often, grew increasingly gloomy. The rain had amused him at first, then annoyed him, but now, in some mimetic effect, it made him as dreary and monotonous as it was. The rain, like a catastrophe, stupefied him, sapped his will to fight, to understand, to adapt. It took away his reason for being and his attempts at irony did not liberate him in the slightest. My father was but a shadow of himself, a veritable wet hen who preferred not to step forward, to keep silent, who brushed off our gestures of kindness as tiresome and, worst of all, seemed to be getting used to his state.

When the sun, conqueror of fog and the last drizzles, finally made its wheezing appearance and shed a bit of light, my father, his face already vindicated from injuries and humiliations, slipped the small bag with the darts into his pocket, watching me with a look that soothed all stings. Thirty minutes later, we were beneath the beech tree, ripe for fantasies, our bodies ready—despite the soggy ground into which each step sank a little deeper—for the marvels they'd been deprived of for so long. Our rituals and games overflowed with a vibrant joy that made our laughter echo and lent our songs a note of wildness. Almost half way between the car and the farmhouse, as we pursued our unaltered challenges and scattered our protestations of love at the feet of the trees, a deluge, frigid and raging, burst down upon us. What a trek through the depths of the forest! Bushes became walls, branches fortifications. We waded through mud. We barely advanced. To regain a bit of courage, I told stories in which we had to maintain the elegance of a musketeer, the valour of an explorer, the impassiveness of a secret agent. For the very first time, I discovered that appealing to the imagination enables you to overcome difficult situations. I didn't yet know that imagination not only allows you to confront moments of horror or shock but also makes existence possible, even bearable and that with its help we can laugh about serious things and make the ridiculous serious.

I crossed the threshold of the farmhouse inn a hero to the acclaim of Régine and Floriane, who immediately took me into their heavy arms and pressed me to their vibrant flesh. But I was shivering. I needed other kinds of attention. In the bathroom, Régine sat next to me as I bobbed in the warm water of the bathtub. She lathered up an orange-scented soap, then rubbed her hands along my body, which she said was as soft as the buds and new leaves of spring. She said little. She covered me with kindness. The back and forth of Régine's hands on my arms, my legs, my torso, my stomach evoked a pleasure I sensed was becoming too visible and which the proximity of this beautiful woman's breasts, swelling beneath her blouse, damp in spots, was aggravating. I was vulnerable. When I wanted to turn away to hide my attraction, Régine prevented me. She didn't laugh, didn't tease me. She knelt down and slipped her hands under my body to lift me slightly out of the water. Being so powerless thrilled me. Régine bent her head forward so I could learn, without fear and without haste, how certain desires are sated. Steeped in modesty, in the rapture this bath brought me, I had forbidden myself to speak about it with anyone at all. Nonetheless, I often let the black comb I'd stolen from Régine, peek out of my pocket.

Scoffing at attachments. Having spices harvested around the world at my fingertips. Having particles from all over the world on my eyelids. Hearing, in my inner ears, interlacing melodies and words that catch fire. Sensing the coolness of rivers and streams that flow in all directions. Feeling the life of winds and the scent of trees on my skin. And in order to avoid being defeated from the start, resolving—for the sake of your beautiful eyes—to make it all prolific!

The Fruit Platter

All my mother knew was this: the man was a famous magician, my father had met him in the newsroom of a newspaper and invited him to lunch, they would both arrive in less than an hour. My brothers and I looked at each other with joy and trepidation. A magician! In flesh and blood! A magician in our home with whom we could discuss unsolved problems, obscure obstacles, and the swarms of misunderstandings that plague children's brains. We had to gather quickly what we knew, open our only book of magic tricks, a manual relegated to the bottom of a trunk after we tried our hands at a few novice tricks. No! That would be ridiculous! Our role should be limited to watching what the magician would not fail to make appear or disappear before our very eyes. Each in his place. And no pretence!

A priori, the magician—short, rather slight, hair stuck to his head—did not have a striking physique but his noble bearing and calm elegance proved that even without getting close to people or things, he saw and heard everything. What a privilege to visit with those around you in such an intimate way, to follow the paths of their thoughts, to stroll through their dreams and along the shores of their fantasies! Passing the bureau in the front hall, the magician said: *I don't know where this statue came from, I see only its regenerative power.* Then he turned towards us, the children, and I was certain he wanted to know who was responsible for the severed head, even though the scar from when my father glued it back together was almost invisible. The magician had no trouble deciphering what I surely wasn't hiding well and gave me an understanding smile that was both sublime and unbearable, a smile I would rediscover two decades later, completely unexpectedly, in the Mandralisca Museum in Cefalù, and of which I wouldn't have had the slightest memory if I had not suddenly found myself in front of Antonello da Messina's *Portrait of an Unknown Man*—a face illuminated by malice with certainly the most mocking lips ever painted. The magician displayed this very same smile on discovering who had perpetrated the decapitation. But the most admirable thing about this man, whom no degree of distress could move, was his voice. My entire body was susceptible to its octaves of sensuous and comforting sounds that dispelled the darkness with an efficiency that merchants and priests would have reason to envy! The conversation during the meal was as much about magic and ghosts, spectres and illusions as it was about words, their resonance, their flesh, how to tame them, how to establish a relationship with them, how to distance oneself from them and then approach them again. The magician who had the indulgence and clarity of a sage, initially became more enigmatic, then adopted a disquieting gravity when he evoked several words (without saying them) which evince such vulgarity, horror or malevolence, yet can't be slain or burnt, that they should at the very least be kept mum, never pronounced, to keep them from defiling us. As the magician said this, it seemed some suffering had sequestered him, because he would not look at any of us, the muscles in his neck tensed spasmodically, his saliva had trouble passing down his throat, and I was certain that his body temperature had fallen at least two degrees. What evil spells was he fighting against? . . . What tormentors were besetting him? . . . The silence that followed his declaration weighed on us. No one said a word and we didn't know where to find refuge. A vague fear disheartened us and smothered our earlier liveliness and delight. My mother, perhaps realizing it was best to take advantage of the magician's distractedness, had the strength to ask him what these terrible words were. The magician tugged at the skin of his lower jaw with both hands and in a voice *in extremis,* he pronounced the four words . . . then his voice caught. With dazzling speed, the magician came to his senses, that is, his face became calm again and the suavity returned to his voice. He then told us stories of volcanoes to dispel the dreaded episode. But the impression remained strong: the four words had terrorized me, as if I had been holding in my hand a ball of poison that was lethal on mere contact. I learnt what the words meant. I learnt their reality. And for years afterwards, if I ever heard some naïf say one of the forbidden words, I pictured the suffering, the failures and illnesses that would certainly befall that unfortunate individual. It took a great deal reflection and reading before I dared face those four words, before I dared say or write them, before I finally shook off the magician's jinx . . . To each his own fate! To each his own slings and arrows!

While the incident of the four words troubled the meal, I still didn't realize that the magician's pronouncements would play a central role in my life. Having been informed of our guest's visit only at the last minute, my mother hadn't had time to prepare a dessert and at the end of the meal, she placed on the table the enormous platter my parents had bought in a village in Sicily crossed by a highway used by thousands of lorries that shook the buildings and barely missed crushing us every time we stepped outside. Since the platter, magnificently laden with fruit, was closest to me, I was invited to serve myself first, a privilege I did not want to pass up. I didn't realize just how invincible a mask of impassivity can make us whereas displaying emotions can render us vulnerable. In a few seconds, it was clear to everyone that I was examining the fruit without discretion, trying find the one I deserved most, to spot, for example, the plumpest, most golden, most beautiful plum, the one the gods, to whom I didn't give a single thought, had reserved for me. My mother quickly stiffened and ordered me to take the piece of fruit that was closest to me, the closest one and no other. When you're defenceless, when you're hiccupping in dismay, you don't usually have a magician come to the rescue! With his voice that banished all discord, that swallowed any resistance, the magician turned to me and said: *Always choose the best fruit.* Who could defy such invulnerability? . . . I put the apple I was holding back on the platter and in a moment of delight that no words could tarnish, a moment of infinite depth, I chose a Mirabelle plum and I recall its taste to this day—a sweetness that will never fade nor will I tire of it.

Did you know that acts of kindness never abolish fears? . . . That kindness does not absolve us of anything? . . . Look at the chandelier over our heads. Look at its light. It's not familiar to you. It's the light of times past. It's the light of candles that the phantoms who whisper in our ears don as halos.

The Cast-Iron Pan

If my brothers came into the kitchen while my mother was cooking a meal, she would send them about their business in a voice that brooked no opposition. For them, the kitchen was off limits, but I was often invited to stay and watch her follow recipes, from the first step to the last. I was eight years old and unsure if my status merited envy or contempt, but as soon as I realized I enjoyed it, I no longer cared if my brothers envied or mocked me. The realm of the kitchen had been conferred on me—such was fate!

Before setting to work, I had to protect my clothes with an apron purchased from a boutique in a chic part of town—a red apron on the front of which a hen strutted with her four chicks. My mother had let me choose between it and two others, one decorated with daisies, the other with a big heart. In the first kitchen sessions, my role was limited that of observer, yet I soon proved useful, not just as a kitchen hand who could peel and chop the vegetables but one also able to master more complicated techniques. For example, when I was nine, I could take over the preparation on my own of a mushroom risotto, an *émincé de veau*, or a cherry clafoutis, and I no longer confused the words 'marmiton', 'mirliton', 'maquignon', 'martagon', 'mirepoix' or 'mero'. My mother marvelled at my prodigious skills and would rail against the majority of modern girls who were incapable of doing anything, who could neither cook nor even speak proper French, which made them inferior in her eyes to the very condition they wanted to escape. My mother smiled, joyfully offered advice and clear explanations, sometimes she lifted me onto a chair so I could see things from above. She wanted me to taste the sauces before she did, to be able to recognize herbs and spices. She ran her hand through my hair, hugged me for a few seconds with a laugh that was free of guile. Our time in the kitchen, in this retreat where nothing weighed on us and where we lacked for nothing, was one of kindness and affection. However, on rare occasion, my mother, forgetting everything, would fix her eyes on me like a strict governess and, in a voice filled with menace and magic, she would announce: *A girl who is ashamed of liking to cook is a halfwit, a Maritornes fit for a*

109

beating. That won't happen to you. I did not answer. I learnt new words—like Maritornes—and hid my unease with questions that started to flow the moment I needed them: Why is it more complicated to make vanilla cream than chocolate cream? Why do purple runner beans turn green when cooked, why does dough rise when it's resting, why does lemon juice cure foods? . . . Why, why, why? . . . Afraid of difficult situations, I had collected a stock of questions I wrote down in a yellow notebook so I wouldn't forget them. Except for these precarious moments that left me dreading the panicked state of an imposter exposed, our times in the kitchen were filled with an atmosphere of confidence, encouragement and love. In those moments, my mother loved me. Being loved was possible. I savoured these moments that banished any sombre shadows or oppressive worries. Just her and me. Like two accomplices . . .

One Sunday morning when we were preparing a large dinner, the older of my two brothers came into the kitchen for a glass of lemonade, shattering the intimacy in which my mother wanted to envelop the two of us. The innocent zeal of this guilty incursion. I saw my mother drop a teaspoon and, in a voice of equal parts sweetness and authority, she asked my brother to pick it up. Just as he bent down, my mother took the cast-iron pan, the one I could barely lift with two hands, and held this pan a foot and a half above my brother's head. When he stood up, he hit his head so hard that he gave a yelp of pain and immediately started to cry, he who was so disgusted by tears, he who had always been spared them. My mother dabbed his head with a damp cloth, telling him it wasn't serious, and took him back to his room so he could rest. I was stunned. I didn't have the slightest doubt my mother had held the heavy pan there on purpose, betraying my brother's trust—her favourite son. No! It couldn't be! Had she gotten lost in a daydream, one of those fictions she loved so deeply, forgetting the danger the pan presented? . . . Had she not been able to turn fast enough . . . Mere conjectures. I wore myself out going over what I'd witnessed in minute detail. My mother's return would disperse my speculations.

She lifted me up and sat me on the counter so our eyes were at the same level. She held my waist— and I could feel her nails against my sides—she brought her face close to mine—I could feel her breath in my mouth—and she delivered, in a voice that shreds all will, that puts an end to any struggle, she delivered the sentence I'm not about to forget, delivered it like a verdict, a curse intended to isolate each person from what he sees in another, to turn friend, lover, brother into a rival or a tormentor, she delivered this sentence that, true or false, desolates, rots the soul: *You must always, at every moment, distrust everyone around you . . . Even your father . . . And even your mother . . .*

You press your fist against my nose and say: I hate men of principle. Principle is the opposite of thought, of reflection. You say: Principles kill doubt; they destroy life. You add: I love you because you are not a man of principle. You lift your fist off my nose and you smile.

The Model Airplanes

I never gave the slightest sign of my indifference. On the contrary! The more my collection grew, the more the passion appeared to dominate me! A veritable jumble of false smiles, feigned joy, as if it were necessary to mask what lacerates, to hide it behind pantomimes of rapture. Twiddling with cheap junk! . . . How many hours wasted? . . . How many afternoons spent not reading books, not playing outside, not walking along streets in which you come across faces that fill you with joy and people you can engage in conversation, real or imagined? . . . Seated on my desk chair, the pieces all spread out before me, the instruction manual with its wicked print unfolded on my knees, I assembled, I built, I tweaked, I painted with miniscule brushes, I constructed an impressive bellicose aerial fleet that my finicky brain perfected. For several Christmases and birthdays—because my brothers loved them and told everyone they did—my father gave me two or three model airplane kits to build, jetfighters and bombers that were shown on the box lids flying invincibly through cataclysmic settings. Nothing aggravated me more than this highly regulated order, this minutiae, the attention and constant worry over details that had to be mastered in order for the result to be excellent, for the Spitfire Mk XVI not to embarrass the Royal Air Force and for the German Stuka Ju 87 to appear as menacing as ever. Out of sheer perversity, I persisted in trying to improve. The slightest imperfection was intolerable and I absolutely had to finish, even if it meant sacrificing even more time, deciding, for example, to disassemble what I'd just put together to reassemble the motor in a stricter fashion with a purist's exactitude since the motor was generally hidden and no one would ever have noticed any defect. I had heard the model builder's supreme happiness lay in knowing that what was hidden under the *casing* was close to perfection, the very perfection I strove for and was repelled by. This happiness seemed to me to be the most hollow, the saddest happiness one could feel. I pursued it. A burden of irony not without its share of voluptuousness! Only my mother deplored these building sessions, which she believed to be unhealthy and capable of deforming children's brains in order to turn them into docile instruments for the worst kind of dirty work. I could have told her everything.

I could have admitted the extent to which these airplanes made me desolate; how building them devastated me. I could have confessed that when I engaged in this frigid activity, I often felt the walls of my room contract until they left only a narrow cell in which there was just enough space for me to suffer my hard lot, that is, to continue these triturations of a maniacal child that leave no room for the soul. But admitting this felt repugnant!

On my thirteenth birthday, for the sixth year in a row, my father gave me planes to build while my brothers were given gifts that encouraged them to escape outdoors. I smiled. I didn't try to revolt or show my displeasure.

The next day, I was surprised to feel a tide of rage swelling inside that I didn't know what to do with and which I had to release one way or another. I didn't resent my father—I could have passed him without uttering a single word of reproach—my fury was aimed far beyond a specific act or person, it arose from with the necessity of having to share the air with others, with the discovery that there are no inhabitants on this earth, just cohabitants. I put my entire collection of model planes on my bed. I turned my bed into an international airport from which all the airplanes could take off, even the enemy aircraft, even those that only meet in the air to shoot each other down. The Messerschmitt Bf 109s sat nicely next to the Fokker G.Is whose tails cost me hours of nightmares and anxiety. No more dissembling! My cry of rage had to find its form, to burst! One after the other, with no hierarchy in my aversion, I tossed each airplane out of the window. Not a single one flew. Not one of them managed even a semblance of flight, at best, one or two of them sketched a few senseless arcs, a few mindless tailspins, before crashing nose-first into the earth. The moment each plane hit the ground, I was filled with a consoling joy that I immediately wanted to renew. Ten minutes of frenzy were enough to destroy my air force, that is to say, the memory of days filled with the tedium and misery I both detested and desired.

Down in the courtyard, my vanity was rather flattered to see that a few of my constructions had withstood the six-story fall, but the sentiment didn't last long. I gathered the crumbs of my fleet into a large clear plastic bag. Back in the apartment, I hung the bag of apocalyptical debris from the dining room ceiling. From that point on, there was no longer any question of model kits, of airplanes, of model airplanes.

Hanging in the closet are my mother's dresses. My mother is not afraid of vivid colours—yellow, orange, green, red—but she has a marked preference for shades of purple and burgundy. Strips of colour undulate, billow, awaiting the flesh over which they will be draped. But what reaches us from them, creeping and tenacious, is the smell of my mother's body. It wafts towards in protest . . . in protest against death, death that has already come.

My Mother's Tears

My mother did not cry when my brothers were born: the birth of a first son and all the joy that comes with it; the birth of a second son and all the joy that comes with that. Joy simply released, without the shadow of a tear or pretence. Pure joy, crystal clear.

The bath water is covered with suds. I must be six years old at the most. I'm standing in a bathtub filled with water. My mother is lathering me with soap. She plays with the soap on my body, draws a spiral that starts from my belly button and rises in circles to my mouth. She takes more lather and draws stripes. She tells me I'm her prisoner. She takes another handful of lather and made a rounded pile and says it's the prisoner's ball and chain. She wipes everything away and kisses my stomach, my chest, my neck, my shoulders, and we laugh. Her kisses on my stomach make us laugh the most. She points her two index fingers at my nipples then pokes them. She pinches my sides to make me squirm, she blows into my armpits, she prods my wrists, she devours my eyes, she teases my throat, she mouths my navel, she pinches my palms, she pretends to delouse me, she says we're overdoing it, she turns me around easily and wipes a washcloth down my back then over my bottom. I hear the word 'callipygian' for the first time. She nibbles my buttocks, telling me they smell good. And then my mother washes my hair.

There's a lot of steam in the bathroom. The mirror on the medicine cabinet no longer reflects anything. My mother starts combing my hair, telling me a story in which my skull is a meadow and each hair a blade of grass which contains a second of happiness. I try to guess how many hairs I have on my head and how many days of happiness that represents. I have long hair. Just like hers. I feel the comb in my hair, the teeth of the comb touch my skull with the exact amount of pressure, that is, not too soft and not too hard, an expert touch. Yes, my mother combs my hair with expertise. She massages my skull, rubbing each parcel of skin, her fingertips like beneficent pads. And the pressure of her fingers calms me, almost put me to sleep, then her fingers reach the nape of my neck, the first vertebra of my spine, they linger and move down to the second, the third. I wait for her fingers to travel all the way down my backbone but they make a detour, shift to my left shoulder and there, instead of rubbing, instead of caressing, her fingers clench at my skin, as stiff as spikes. Her nails suddenly jab, scrape my skin, back and forth, wounding me. I say nothing. I don't cry. My life contracts into this pain. And my mother's nails persist, meticulously, like hooks carved specifically to dig into flesh, to mangle, mutilate, ravage it. I picture the blood on my mother's nails. Would she like to lick it off? Would she like to watch it dry on her hands? Would she like to smear it over my face? . . . Small specks trouble the water. I wonder if it's soap, dirt, dirty soap. The nails are becoming irritated. No torture will wring a moan from me. I know the pain, but it doesn't touch me. My mother turns me around brusquely. Her face is pale, her cheeks covered with the tears I did not shed.

Things that torment others or cause them anxiety, that reduce them to silence or fill them with fear, that make them talk, make them tell everything, can leave others completely indifferent. Those who have an elephant's hide know nothing of the stones' temperature or that of sand. They go through life with chests like bunkers. For their imaginations to come to life, they need orgies, bloodbaths, axes sticking out of heads, bungee jumping, amusement parks, natural disasters with a hundred thousand victims.

The Cloth Handkerchief

When we weren't off on excursions, we stood before the chalet we'd rented for three weeks amid mountains that embraced us from a distance. My mother had declared it impossible that her children not know the scents of the mountains, the air that elevates, the sense of grandeur that surrounds you, and the sense of insignificance that grows within. The mountains were going to educate us. My father made gentle fun of this Swiss moral code. He chalked it up to her possible discovery of some new writer, no doubt an admirer of high peaks that pacify rebel souls and the emptiness that swallows up bad thoughts.

My mother did not disagree.

Because the chalet was isolated, we had to settle for not meeting other people and keeping ourselves busy. My brothers, already grown, used the time to prepare for their exams, while I could sit for hours, lost in thought and gazing at the magnificent land-scape in which nothing sordid could possible exist. At those times I liked to imagine I was skirting eternity or I might walk down to a torrent I'd discovered, in which I would try to hold my feet in the icy water for as long as possible, watching as they turned red, then white, until the pain forced to me to take them out. I had convinced myself that this exercise, like drinking sour milk, would make me much stronger.

Every other day, we would go for a walk, that is, a hike with a specific goal, which required a calculation of the time and means necessary to best reach the destination. I'd have preferred we just wander, changing our itinerary as we went, that we not care about our exact altitude or the idiotic name of this or that mountain in the distance. I hated the moments when my body grew heavy, my feet burnt and I was overcome by that *healthy exhaustion* as my mother liked to parrot. I didn't loathe the feeling so much as the self-satisfied comments it provoked, short remarks always cantered on the well-earned rest and unparalleled repose to come. I would rather we stop as often and for as long a time as we wished. I'd have liked to stretch out next to a stream and abandon our goals for good. But I was the only one who felt this way and I hardly counted. I scowled with dismay and unhappiness, dragging my feet through a landscape that surreptitiously turned gloomy and repellent. I discovered the misery that stifles revolt, elicits renunciation and intensifies as a result.

This slowed our pace, which annoyed my family of walkers determined not to lose sight of their objective, especially my two brothers, who pulled me by the arms and called me *girly girl*. After four days of vacation and two climbs, they had decided to take my fits of melancholy into account as a constant factor or objective danger when calculating the difficulty of this or that ascent. I took a certain pride in this! The number of kilometres, the incline, the weather forecast, the hazardous passages, *my mood*, none of these—as inevitable factors—should be neglected. I endured a few more accusatory grimaces, which soon softened, then nothing more. I have to admit that on the days spent in the chalet, I knew how to don a contemplative expression so in tune with the profundity of the location that it wouldn't have occurred to anyone to suspect me of harbouring any internal rejection of this rigid landscape around us. I had, vis-à-vis this decor, a turbid feeling that kept me from knowing for certain if it had a liberating or an oppressive effect on me, if I should escape or submit.

Towards the end of our stay, they all became excited by an ambitious plan. Our family was to ascend the mountain directly opposite us, to conquer it, besiege it, to avenge ourselves to a certain extent for having had to watch it swallow the sun which was impaled on its peak much too early every afternoon. On this one occasion, I refused to join the hike, not out of nonchalance, fear or sadness, but because I had no desire to experience this mountain in any way other than from the position I had been looking at it. I found this way of relating to the mountain most pleasing, most satisfying. My decision suited everyone: I would guard the chalet while they climbed the mountain. I could even take part in their struggle to reach the summit thanks to the binoculars that hung on the inside of the closet door and which they wanted to leave for me to make good use of ... A bluish dawn had barely broken when, through the small windows in my room, I saw them set off on their adventure, the only movement in the sleeping landscape. I had the entire day to myself and I planned on taking advantage of this in my fashion, that is, in the silence and solitude of my daydreams, devoted to potential acts of imagined bravery. I'd taken the only armchair in the dining room, a comfortable rocking chair, and placed it on the flat stretch of ground right in front of the chalet. I curled up with the intention of not leaving this refuge for an instant. Not taking up any more space . . . Not being any more significant than any individual tree or rock in my field of vision . . . Contemplation, dozing, daydreaming, listening to the flight of a kite, dozing again, more daydreams, being as anonymous as any blade of grass, twig or root—that is what I desired. The cold, like the heat, came in waves, and the variations in temperature woke me. I had a blanket and a bottle of water within reach.

From this perch and indulging in this regenerative rest, I noticed a man making his way up the hill, cutting the grass with a scythe. I could have used the binoculars to stare at him from afar, but that seemed too easy and too cowardly. Besides, the man would come nearer since the edge of the field he was mowing was less than ten metres from the chalet. After an hour, he had reached this border and I could see more and more clearly how the steel blade rose sideways into the air before plunging towards the earth. I was sure that a movement this beautiful and this brutal could solve every problem, vanquish all enemies and cross centuries in a patient and invincible rhythm. The man came up to me and took the bottle of water without a word, but with a look that blended strength with tenderness. I asked him if he had finished his work, if he wanted to drink anything else, if he lived near or far. The man's legs were crooked, his face shrivelled, his skin like bark, his skull squashed beneath hair cut short and his voice contradicted all this. He said he had only to see my laziness in order to share it and if I watched him carefully as he scythed, I wouldn't have to engage in this chore to feel all of its sensations. I listened to his radiant, radiating voice, a sensual and enchanting voice you immediately wanted to attach yourself to. Words stripped themselves bare in his mouth and came out washed clean, intact, like chimes, beyond usefulness or uselessness, liberated from fear and seduction.

When the man had walked off a few metres, I took advantage of the moment to look closely at the scythe he had left propped up against the wall of the chalet. The blade fascinated me, thwarted my sense of reason. Did the steel reflect the world, my face, my nightmares, obsessive fears, hopes or impossible visions? . . . I shivered. I put my right index finger on the top of the blade, I pressed rather firmly and

swept along the blade quickly for a dozen centimetres. Looking at the flesh of my first finger sliced to
the core, I experienced neither fear nor pain but a
blinding sense of emptiness and solitude. When the
man saw me, he said nothing. He first tied his cloth
handkerchief under the wound before patting my
cheeks. After several minutes he took a flask from
his pocket and sprinkled the cut. That the bleeding
stopped so quickly did not astonish me. The man
also took a glass jar of ointment from his pocket. If
I wanted the scar to disappear, I would have to stick
my finger in the cream that smelt of flowers. The
man's voice, like a benevolent shadow, comforted
me. Nothing in the sequence of events could have
been more fitting. The man bestowed a look of trust
on me and left with traces of my blood on his scythe
and on the handkerchief he left behind.

You take a twig and snap it in two, you take a glass and drop it, you take a book and tear it apart, you take a piece of cloth and rip it, you take a light bulb and break it, you take a coffee pot and scratch it, you take an egg and crush it. You say: *These sounds are almost nothing, but we can also decide at which moment noises will reach us by accident.*

The Plug

I never got used to it but I also didn't refuse to go,
past the city limits, outside all geography, to the
building whose roughcast walls gave it an ailing air.
It was the asylum. There, for three years, lived
Fabien, a cousin who was my age and whose physical strength was impressive. When we were little, we
had played together under the watchful eyes of the
birches and a nettle tree in my aunt and uncle's
garden. We were an odd pair: he was robust and
talkative, I rather frail and quiet. Fabien liked to
show me his biceps, his wooden pistols, his card-
board crowns, his collection of squirrel tails, and
how well his jaws worked. He drew me into fits of
laughter we redoubled for no reason and prolonged
simply in response to the day's joy. Innocent in
appearance, we advanced along the same paths.
Fabien didn't frighten me. I liked him. When we
fought—fighting with him, I learnt how to defend
myself—he was always careful not to wound me and

if I ever pretended to be hurt, a wild sorrow filled his face. I would dispel his panic with a smile.

When he was eleven, after he had let loose all the cows on a dairy farm in the dead of winter, mimicking the cries of Alpine herders, and then showed no remorse. Fabien was placed, for his parents' peace of mind and everyone's safety, in a secure place, in the asylum, that building with roughcast walls. So that no one could claim we were neglecting him, we would visit Fabien every month or two, sometimes the entire family, sometimes just my mother and me. As soon as I stepped into the entrance hall, I would hear a crackling I couldn't place and I would stare fixedly at the old woman who was always seated next to the reception desk, a crazy woman, immobile in her green housecoat. The skin on her nose and around her eyes was covered with warts, warts so enormous and so numerous I was certain that her face would one day disappear under the clusters of protuberances, unless there did exist, as the tales I was still reading at the time implied, various balms, elixirs and flowers that grew only on certain mountains you could pick only at great risk of life and limb, or else magic words you only had to pronounce, all of which could restore to the old woman not only smooth, healthy skin but also the complexion of a young girl that would defy death more effectively than love.

I traced the many nicks and notches on the walls with my fingers as I climbed the stairs. On the fourth floor, at the end of a hallway lit by nightlights whose glow fell mostly on metal chairs, was Fabien's room. Seated or stretched out on his bed, his gaze lost in the void, my cousin was losing weight. He no longer laughed. He understood that he had been betrayed. Did he forgive me my inability to get him out? . . . I would have liked to spread a fog throughout the asylum, a mist that would put everyone to sleep for several minutes, the nurses, the guards and the visitors. Taking advantage of this gentle conjuration, I would take Fabien by the hand and lead him to a hillside I knew, a mound on which bodies, lying languidly on sparse grass, sheltered from all threats and worries, protected from love and hate, give themselves up as offerings. But could he have managed the climb? . . . Fabien was suffering, yet he was utterly indifferent to his suffering. When he agreed to take a short walk with us, to trot along the gravel path that crossed the park, he refused to remove the two fingers he always kept stuck in his mouth.

Every two weeks at first, then once a month, Fabien's parents drove him home, dragged him out on the lake, to the mountains, onto the carousel, to the circus, but as soon as he left the confines of the asylum, Fabien became so violent, capable of destroying any object, of breaking any rule, that his parents spaced out their visits even more. The room at the end of the fourth floor corridor in the asylum with the roughcast walls eventually became the sole locus of his life.

One afternoon when we came to see him and he wasn't in his room, my mother went to find a nurse for information and I climbed up a flight of stairs and pushed open a door without any sign, certain that Fabien was there. By chance or instinct, I wasn't mistaken. In a room with a high, vaulted ceiling, completely covered in green tile, with showers separated by real walls—also tiled in green—along three sides of the room, I saw Fabien lying in a bathtub placed in the centre of the room filled with soapless water, his body covered with goose bumps. Grimy from hundred years of water that had worn away the enamel, the bathtub terrified me. The water was turning yellow, taking on the colour of the rust. I helped Fabien get out and stood him under a shower. The tub, the tomb of the end of the world, expanded, filled my head. I edged closer and pulled out the rubber plug attached to a thin, broken chain. I

watched the water disappear down the drain and felt
sadness rise in me, because what was disappearing—
I understood without knowing—was the fate of men,
the blood of soldiers, the shame, the fears, the com-
motions, the self-satisfaction, the nights of love, the
illusions, insults and illness, the girls we long for, the
words we believe, the praise and the lies, what truly
matters, the friends who love you, those who betray
you, the enthusiasms, the tears of joy . . . yes, what
disappeared at the bottom of this bathtub, was
human life, my own life, suddenly reduced to a few
drops of dirty water with no effect on anything . . .
And while the water drained away, I stuffed the
plug—black but covered with white traces of lime—
in my pocket, without thinking. No other object, no
sight better symbolized the horror than this plug
stolen from a bathroom, the place where Fabien
would die, a gunshot in his mouth.

.

Everything's moving in my head. I try not to think of anything. The titles of books and entire sentences reach me. One after another. They don't disappear until I consider the strength of their meaning. I don't read to recognize myself in the books. As I light a cigarette, I have to reconcile myself to lost illusions, to look homeward angel, to I have no childhood memories, to eat chocolates: *Little girl, eat chocolates, you see, all the religions in the world won't teach you any more than a candy store, eat, little piggy, eat*!

And there you are, eating chocolates!

The Ex-Voto

The fashion for scooters must rely on the regular appearance of ever-lighter and more practical models. These days scooters seem indestructible even though you can fold them up. The only one we ever owned at home was elegant, painted an intense shade of blue, but ancient and hard to steer because it was so heavy. Although she never forbade it, my mother did not like to see me take the scooter out on the streets. She claimed the toy didn't suit me, that it made her nervous to know I was on that plank with no protection and she simply could not abide the thought of having to take me to the hospital for stitches on God knows which part of my body (forehead, elbow, knee, groin or eyebrow) for a cast on God knows which bone, the names of which she enunciated in a voice that honed each one to a point: humerus, radius, cubitus, femur, tibia, malleolus, rotula. This convinced me that it was enough to evoke a reality for it to come into existence, each bone she designated this way poked my flesh, shredded the tissues fiercely and ferociously!

I would sometimes take the scooter, not without a touch of fear, and, riding very prudently to avoid an accident, I would make my way through the city either in search of new passageways and unknown cul-de-sacs—picturing myself evading dastardly pursuers thanks to a hidden door, a manhole, a low wall, an awning, or gutter—or to reach a semi-industrial zone that appealed to me in the outskirts of the city. In this hybrid neighbourhood there were dilapidated family homes, unused warehouses, sheds, three enormous petrol tanks corroded by time, stretches of pointless walls, a brick storehouse next to which stood the remains of a crane, isolated trees and a few recently built factories whose lustre darkened immediately on contact with this rusted universe, rebellious against any attempts at embellishment. Nothing could flourish in this place; its reputation was confirmed before it even came to that! A smell of oil, of welding and of wet iron—not to mention the fumes from a few black puddles that refused to dry up—filled my nose and would have allowed me, blindfolded, to recognize this neighbourhood among all others. Why was I not afraid in this zone where the last vagabonds could find refuge at night and where all sorts of petty thieves, knives on their belts, jaws clenched, went to sink the loot they'd gotten over the last few nights? On foot, I certainly wouldn't have stayed more than five minutes between these sweating walls along which men walked with the gait of the damned, their eyes fixed to the ground ... On my scooter, I felt safe. As I crossed the neighbourhood I had the impression that a dream was constructing the surroundings as I advanced, that I could embrace, without being wounded or flayed, this incomprehensible treasure, charged with lack-lustre sparks and concentrated distress.

Sometimes innocence can ward off disaster and arm itself with boldness. Who could possibly have been interested in me in this world attuned only to danger, gold and the indecent? ... No uncertainty and no weariness could have put an end to my indolent enthusiasm but an image, as fundamental as a slash, swept away my heedless thrills! In the court-yard of a warehouse which had drawn my eye because of its hundreds of broken windows, I saw a giant of a man with short black hair, standing like an angry god in this field of glass and this giant, his arm extended straight out, held a man above the ground and the man whimpered implausible explanations, pointlessly thrashing his short legs. There was a monstrous physical disproportion in this tableau that I had previously seen only in certain comic strips. I stood frozen, dismayed by my inability to speak, to make the slightest gesture, by my powerlessness to stop the humiliation I was forced to witness. The moment the short man turned his wretched face towards me, pleading, taking me for an apparition or an angel-magician, a benevolent demon who could put an end to it all, finally end it, the giant's fist hit him with a blow so powerful, I saw his head explode, that is, blood spattered everywhere, his bones shattered, his lips split, his eyes rolled back in his head. The giant held at arm's length this man gone limp, a marionette's body, and tossed the lifeless body onto the shards of glass like a cheap cut of meat. Fear—despite the tears—beefs up a child's muscles. Fear gave me license to turn my scooter into a racing car without equal. I wanted to get away from that sight as fast as I could so fear wouldn't have time to set down roots, to spread its net of obsession. Faster! Faster! I spurred the scooter on with furious thrusts. I didn't brake in the curves. I poured all my strength into reaching the few houses that marked the border of this cursed zone now off limits to me. Ditch the decor . . . Get rid of it all without compromise . . . Let it fall apart! Let it rot! Get lost in the vagaries of my memory . . . But the

shadow on the road . . . Where did it come from? I
tried to avoid it. A shadow of menace that falls suddenly, like a net of madness. And immediately I fell!
My thoughts out of control! A labyrinth that leads
us astray! A toppling of the creature who refuses to
emerge! You find yourself sterile for a moment, dead,
without memory, a time that will leave traces to be
found later, after . . .

The weight and the sensation of sleep numbed
my body, allowed me to look without being frightened at the woman bending over me. I could see
nothing of her body, hidden by a black dress, only
angular ankles and bony hands, still, her face was
enough for me to contemplate. To say that the
woman was old would be a lie, she was age itself or
death brought briefly to life, a corpse that had
climbed out of its grave to witness my fall with the
eyes of a raptor. Excessively transparent, the
woman's skin was beyond wrinkles, beyond the ages,
skin polished by the years, skin no insult could have
touched, skin that was beyond the human. As the
woman helped me get up, I was surprised by her
strength. Once on my feet, I saw that she was taller
than I'd thought. Blood seeped through my torn
trousers and the pain in my knee made me grimace.
The old woman took me by the hand. I followed her

without question, bound to her by a mute pact, like a fascination that shackles. After a few minutes we arrived in her living space, a vast room that smelt of amber, a room filled with bluish light and with a staircase rising at the back. On a coat rack, amid her clothes, hung a baboon that suddenly scratched its head, all ten fingers twitching mechanically; at its feet, lying among cushions, a litter of puppies nursed and, in homage to several sphinxes placed around the room, white cats posed for eternity. Only the birds in an elaborate iron cage two-metre high made any noise. With these animals, the room seemed to breathe, to exist in a place apart.

My disquiet had another source.

Along the walls, hundreds of silvery objects— featuring organs or limbs of the human body—composed a dozen creatures of varying sizes who served as mysterious guardians. Here and there, on a chair or a table, on the armchair or even on the ground, were more body parts, but real and terrifying! They were made of wax and seemed to be waiting for unnatural grafts. The old woman went up to one of the creatures nailed to the wall and removed a piece, a knee, which she handed me while explaining the purpose of ex-votos and the faith I needed to have if I didn't want to limp for the rest of my life. I listened to her enchantress' voice, able to tame wild animals, to put warriors to sleep, a voice that would prevent me, for the rest of my life, from making fun of any man or woman I'd see praying in a church or making a wish on a falling star or throwing a coin into a fountain or listening raptly to some roadside preacher. I took the ex-voto and shuffled out of the room backwards, eyes alternately on the old woman, the wax pieces, the crazy baboon and the silvery figures. I stepped back until I felt behind me the door-knob in the palm of my hand.

The air outside did not lie.

It froze my sweat.

Although the falling dusk did not interrupt the sounds of the city in the slightest, I limped home, my pants torn, my scooter mangled, with a knee-shaped ex-voto in my pocket and in my buzzing head, a story to tell as best I could so my accident wouldn't cause any alarm or reproaches or awkward questions. To evade my mother, I could count only on the arrangement of words, on my taste for lies. Once again, I would tell her everything and reveal nothing.

You have no idea of the riches that are yours when you dream. I brush my nose along the length of your defenceless body. I breathe in your arm, for example, your neck, your armpit, your clavicle. You turn over slowly. I zigzag across your back, which I've already committed to memory. The scents vary from one night to the next, but the smells of biscuit, of slate, of tree resin and pinecones are constant.

The Cup of Sawdust

She brought the book into my room. She sat down next to me, put her arm around my waist, her face gentle, confident of the pleasant accord to come. She pointed at the image with the tip of her smooth, convex nail, a nail that could have been photographed to advertise a brand of perfume associated with the beauty and care of customers' hands, a nail so perfect that my own, although neither gnawed at nor dirty, suddenly seemed repugnant to me. She spoke in an affectionate tone, in a voice above passion and well versed in wisdom. First, she spoke of the light surrounding the Christ child, unreal, celestial. She spoke of the fearless baby playing with an eaglet and looking at another child. She spoke also of the priest or doctor, the one prepared to carry out the operation skilfully with two or three strokes of the blade. How reassuring! Such proof! An image sprang from my mother's words and, the alarm bells fell silent, my fears were soothed. How could she know so many things and still have such youthful cheeks? . . . How could she have retained both a high level of knowledge and such inviting skin, worth braving more or less chivalrous feats, ruses, strategies and battles? . . . I watched my mother, terrifying in her beauty, elegant in her erudition, as she left the room with a gait not even the most determined could imitate, saying with a gently mocking smile that medicine certainly hadn't regressed since Pontius Pilate, that there were absolutely no grounds for fear, and that my sense of reason, if we had to resort to that—and this 'that' stunned me, one small word pronounced in a tone that held hours of worry and hours of suffering and hours loathing for that very worry; my child's sense of reason was developed enough to discern the pairs of opposites to which adults tried to reduce the world: the heavy and the light, the weak and the strong, the ugly and the beautiful, the brave and the cowardly, the sacred and the profane—my sense of reason would have to fight against its own distractions, wipe them out, reduce them to nothing.

I had always hated going to the paediatrician, to that dull ochre house—its arrogant discretion obvious even from a great distance—situated at the end of an alley of arborvitae planted like gallows, devoid of any charm despite the two dogwoods whose name did nothing to lessen my annoyance and exasperation. The ceremony had to be performed: the maudlin doorbell with two tones, the nurse's face on which stagnated an expression of benevolence, an expression that made her treat children like simpletons, the waiting room furnished with plastic benches and decorated with posters of animals (horses and dolphins, but never geese, cows or dromedaries), the doctor's fraternal handshake, his man-of-the-world smile, the ritual of undressing so the auscultation could begin, the throat clearing of the one who looked at my body merely as a body, no more, no less, simply as raw material, a source of livelihood topped by a face that would be better off cooperating and wiping away that despondent and disdainful look.

Where could I find comfort? . . . What daydream might offer relief from this jolting of my soul? . . . A yes or a no from the paediatrician would decide the outcome, radiant in one case, impossible in the other! Although I would rather have wept on my mother's chest, then seasoned her hair with my tears, I had to hide my alarm, I had to be the perfect child, calm and confident, the image of the son she would consent to love. The sentence that would bring deliverance, the

147

one that would arrange everything, would keep me from collapsing under the weight of so many crepuscular visions simply by being spoken—I wondered if there were such a phrase, if there was the slightest chance it would be revealed to me. What should I do? . . . Should I pray, conjure, reason? . . . Should I keep quiet and surround myself with an impassable trench that would prevent the enemy from gaining any hold? . . . Foundering and uncertainty.

More than once, alone in the apartment, I withdrew into the library to look more closely at the picture. I, too, wanted to auscultate! I pulled out the book, shelved under the letter 'P', and opened it to the page with the reproduction of 'The Circumcision', a painting my mother decreed more effective than any tranquilizer, a pick-me-up and restorative in one. That a painter might bear a name which was almost the same as that of the cheese we grated on our pasta did not strike me as droll nor did it calm the shivers that ran down my spine when I looked at the picture. Maybe my mother wasn't lying, maybe I should imitate the Christ child and show the same confidence, and put myself without moodiness into benevolent hands, that is, entrust the most intimate part of my body to well-meaning hands that would banish all future pain. But what if they were trying to trick me? . . . My mother and I were not looking at the same picture, of this I was certain, because she forgot the essential part, she forgot the faces surrounding the Christ child, the figures squeezed tight together with expressions of terror, torment, resignation and bad faith. I considered these figures accomplices in the abominable trap laid out for a child much too young to realize what lay in store for him, despite the fact that he was looking not at the eaglet but at the pillar . . . The sacrificial pillar.

I was six years old! I didn't want anyone to touch my foreskin or to cut it. And they weren't going to alter my refusal by invoking mysterious illnesses meant to justify this violent act. I wanted nothing to do with circumcision. I wanted to forget this terrible word that filled me with dread (those three 'c's horrified me as much as three sickles), this word that had to be contained, stifled, muzzled, strangled. Faced with this word, I could only think of one other word valiant enough to take the brunt, to counter it: secession. At night, I thought of ways to flee the apartment, of towns and countryside I could lose myself in, of how to get hold of the gold ingot my parents kept on top of their wardrobe, of the things I'd have to take with me. I also thought of places I could sleep: in building basements, in cabins in the woods, in houses under construction, uncomfortable places in which the first night is exciting but the following nights drive you to despair. Running away wouldn't just happen! I was right at the age of tiny exploits, escapades without panache. It would be better not to betray my dreams of adventure and prestige, not to reduce them to a few hours of roaming. The solution had to be found at home, had to spring from my child brain, young as I was.

The day before the decisive visit to the paediatrician, the day the decision would be made whether to operate or not operate, to circumcise or not to circumcise, I was holding my penis with my fingers, on the lookout for a solution, the momentum of my thoughts was stopped short by the sight of the red cup filled with sawdust I'd put on the windowsill long ago, but through some devilry had now appeared on my chest of drawers to test me, to tangle everything I'd been toiling to unwind. I went up to the cup and stuck two fingers into the sawdust I'd brought home a few months earlier since our town had a sawmill, not far from the centre, a magical meeting place late certain afternoons, a place where conflicts that could tear apart children between the ages of six and ten were settled and where we could start our favourite games over and over again as long we wanted.

Once we'd breached the enclosure, we loved taking over this forest of trees—cut into planks and laid flat but still rising to the skies—with our games of hide-and-seek, next to which all other games of hide-and-seek were boring, as this grid allowed for the most remarkable ruses and strategies. Yet what drew us even more strongly had no name, a game without heads or tails that began the moment one of us said clearly, though without raising his voice: *sawdust fight*. The term, repeated by all who heard it, allowed each of us to pick up the call but keep it from escaping the confines of the sawmill and alerting passers-by to what we were up to. We went to the sliding door of one of the two hangars in the centre of the compound and, one after the other, like a skulk of foxes, we slipped under the door at a point where the slope of the ground left a small gap. Inside, in full anarchy and with screams of joy, the battle was unleashed and we began shoving each other into the heaps of sawdust piled there. After five minutes, the battle continued with leaps and helter-skelter dives that muddled the notion of adversaries. No tears or injuries hindered our fun: our assassinations were always gentle!

It was a little girl who always kept to the side, clapping her hands in delight at our cavorting spectacle, who saw it first, lit up by a ray of the setting sun. Aghast, we looked in silence at the severed toe, pale white, more waxen than real, a dead digit, the result no doubt of an accident that had taken place in the room where the workers sawed the trunks into planks. The toe mutilated our exhilaration. It spoke of disquiet and death. The era of sawdust battles was over. I filled my pockets with sawdust and at home, I poured it into a cup I then placed on my windowsill. What sorcery had moved it? . . . Who was playing a trick on me just when I most needed clarity and courage to come up with a statement that would shake off the paediatrician, a gesture to ward off all those who sever prepuces? . . . I pictured the toe again. My horror superimposed my member over the toe. My member replaced the toe. It was my member that the little girl saw on the ground, in the sawdust, exactly what the paediatrician was going to slice off in his execution chamber. I sweated through the night without sleeping. A crushing night. Preying on my mind. There was no one to embrace me, to calm my shudders. Before dawn, I locked myself in the bathroom. I perspired under the cool water, my body hidden beneath the suds, immobile until I took my penis in hand and began to pull back the recalcitrant skin. I had to do it. And I did. Afterwards, I pushed the skin back in place. For an hour, as if toughening myself up, I repeated the same up and down motion, not letting my face betray any sign of pain. Naked in front of the paediatrician, I proved to him that everything worked perfectly. I had barely escaped circumcision.

I've caressed women I thought I loved with the feeling I was wounding their skin, soiling their falsely loved lips, with the feeling also of encumbering the folds of their beauty with the arrogance of my sex. My fingers spread traces of death on their skin, leaving ashes behind. I was with these women, yet was not there. And if their bodies arched, it was under the illusion of desire. My desires had not yet become flesh.

My Mother's Tears

She sat before the hairdresser, upright, her back slightly arched, her head dropping back, her eyelids lowered. I was approaching her and could sense a sadness taking root inside her, yet did not shy away from confronting whatever was afflicting her. My only concern was how to place my hand on her shoulder so that she would feel my hand's attentiveness, maybe even its power to heal her wounds, to collect her woes and disperse them. The thought of that power guided my steps. Outside on the window, a snail climbed, glued to the glass, leaving a trail of slime. What faith guided that pilgrim? On what mission had he set off? . . . All I had to do was open the window, pick up the snail without looking at it, without admiring the attributes of its shell, and squeeze it. Its shell would have cracked, its body foaming, hardening, then going slack, and it would all have been over. Out of boredom or disillusion, a sinister, mischievous god would cut the snail's quest short, and this god would have been nothing other than a twelve-year-old boy going to meet his mother. Our existence—with its accumulating days, season upon season, with the burden of successes and failures, of indignations that weaken, that recur, with the indifference that undermines incentive and passion—our existence marches on, but does it leave a trace more elevated, more interesting or exciting than trails of mucus on glass? . . . Is there another god looking down on us, ready to break off our lives for the fun of it? . . . Indigence of faith and thought!

My mother didn't move.

Didn't hear me.

A winter sun streaked the room like white reflections on the white of her skin. I stood behind her, trying to hear her breathe, to see her shoulders rise and fall, but nothing moved. If it had been possible to place a dead woman in this posture, I'd have believed my mother dead. When I put my hand on her shoulder, it didn't quite feel like I was touching a statue—her shoulder did not have the chill of marble, the grain of stone, the humidity of molasse or the dusting of plaster—it also didn't feel like I was touching a body of flesh and blood but, rather, a body of smoke, an immaterial body nothing could reach. My hand on my mother's shoulder began to tremble, to falter. I turned to the window to make sure the snail had disappeared. I could not see any traces of its path.

Like thin bluish green membranes, my mother's eyelids rose. My mother was weeping. Silent tears. A grey shade of dread transformed her face, coated her cheeks with dust, fear dirtied her complexion, blurred the traces of lustre scattered over her cheeks and forehead. She rose and tottered to the centre of the room then began to undress, first her blouse, then her skirt, her black stockings . . . It took time. My mother was like an apparition. An exhausted ballerina. A phantom mother undressing with a heavy slowness over a period of time that seemed an eternity, that resisted being measured. She took off her slip, which slid down the length of her body, a yellow viper that coiled around her feet before she kicked it away. I saw her body ripple next to the pile of clothing that would not settle down as if another body were hidden underneath and I wondered if my real mother were hidden, if she were concealed and a mere reflection were engaging in this ludicrous performance. She took off her brassiere and revealed pointed breasts that I found beautiful. She wiped away a few silent tears, and more came in a slow but constant flood. Again and again, she stroked her legs, her hips, her chest. Her hands ranged over her body in all directions, caressing furiously, as if her hands wanted to take possession of her body, hands that grew more demented in small increments, hands that lunged at her breasts, monstrously, at flesh to be ravaged, violated, and her breasts suffered, their skin turned red, and her hands pulled and twisted, and her breasts bled. Then my mother, as if she had grabbed an offering, came up to me, hands holding her breasts, lifting them slightly, and she said in an agonizing voice: *They're going to cut them off.*

I would like to cover you with feathers, with dirt, with honey, with bark, with ashes, to cover you with laurel leaves, with butterflies, with the colour blue; to cover you with pollen, with resin, with sap, with spices, with quivering, with kisses, with snail shells; to cover you with cheesecloth, with saliva, with hair, with dust, with sawdust, with silk, with breath, with smoke, with larch tree needles. Most of all, I'd like to blanket you with words.

The Ribbon

The longer my hair grew, the more my mother stroked it, the more I wanted to cut it. The memory of the green pumps haunted me. To avoid provoking one of the scenes in which my mother, percussive with anger, always ended up saying—the syllables in her mouth like shards of sound that prick, that pierce—that with short hair I looked like a belligerent little manikin, like a farmer's son without grace or manners. I had to lie each time, explain my embarrassment in gym class, remind her that the fashion for long hair was over, promise I would insist the coiffeur cut off only two or three centimetres, but in any case much less than the last time. By dint of my gentle arguments and repeated promises as well as my expression that masked desire, I would finally convince my mother to give me some money and her consent. I ran down the street as if I were heading off to some distant land, embarking on a voyage that would teach me all there is to know. Swallowing my saliva as fast as I could and tracking my reflection in the shop windows, I ran until pain jabbed at my chest and I arrived panting at Guido's.

Guido, a Sicilian with a majestic voice who wore the same overstitched shirts winter and summer, the same anthracite-coloured trousers and the same shiny shoes, would tell me stories of cunning donkeys or magic olives trees or daredevil dwarves turned into amorphous giants or even of erotic frescos hidden in the basements of sanctuaries and not to be found on any registers or lists. Guido assured me he knew exactly where to find tracks left by angels, the tears of saints, golden thread and vials of blood with magical powers (a drop of this one brings on old age, a drop of that one keeps it away . . .). He told me of a cave in which you can hear the voices of your ancestors and of another where you can listen to famous men argue about the soundness of their actions and the relevance of their theories. He would also tell me stories—and these were my favourite—about his entire family's adventures, those who had succeeded in life and those who had failed, those who believed they had succeeded, those who believed they had failed, and endless stories with various combinations of conspiracy, of trickery, of fortunes won, stolen and lost, of nights of love or venomous hatred, of prayers that save, of vanity and of abandon. He could tell them over and over again as many times as he wished because they were never the same twice. At every intersection, Guido's stories took another turn, barrelled straight ahead, veered off on a tangent, smashed to pieces, re-emerged elsewhere, on a gravel path bordered with fragrant trees or in the middle of an American highway. As soon as I was seated on the leather chair, all I had to do was close my eyes for the stories to flow. I always said the same thing to Guido. It was a request he loved to hear and was enough to cement our friendship: as short as possible but with the illusion of length! Guido made the first snip of his scissors and began talking. He tried his best to satisfy my impossible request whereas I let myself be seduced by his voice with which he interpreted the world in a cascade of words, joyfully talkative, vigorous and extravagant, far from numbers, silence and reasonable measures. His voice made life joyful and crazy!

One afternoon, when I itched with desire for a haircut, my mother, who had honoured my last return from Guido's with an *I'll look at you again once your hair has grown back*, my mother was not to be persuaded. She barely listened to me, remained unmoved or shredded my desires with a mere word or gesture. For more than an hour, with the help of detours, spirals, byways, deviations and linguistic carbuncles, I repeated the necessity of getting my hair cut. I didn't have the strength to dismiss my mother's attitude as negligible, as without impact on me. I could not admit or even formulate the truism that one should never expect anything from others, that hope is a vice, a petty thing you should discard before it anesthetizes you, sweeps you away, saps the joy from your pleasures, however ephemeral they are. In the end, I remained there, standing idiotically in front of an empty aquarium, king of nothing, tragically mortal under the lash, refusing to utter a word, incapable even of shedding a tear or shouting or grabbing my mother by the throat and crushing her windpipe like a crustacean's shell and relishing in the cracking that would put a stop to her disdain.

There was no escape from my distress! . . .

Handed over to fate!

Without showing any more interest in me than in a distraction that might briefly amuse her, my mother set down her book, turned to me and, after a minute or two of silence, said in a smiling, affectionate voice full of engaging calm: *Very well, let's go to the salon!*

Silent in the back seat of the car as we drove past Guido's, I understood that my mother had the choice of weapons. In a neighbourhood with nothing remotely appealing to me, the salon made an effort to impress: the mirrors were framed in pink marble, the floor, black as liquorice, had the consistency of rubber, wall lights in the shape of baboon heads spread a bluish light, a mosaic on the back wall depicted Venus stretched out on a conch shell, being coiffed by a young woman who looked like a harmonious version of the woman at the reception desk who had welcomed us by inscribing something into a register she handled as delicately as if it were the rarest of incunabula. Sitting in a chair that was much too large, already nauseated from the smell of nail polish and perfume, I could see a dozen people bustling about, their faces masks moulded into the most horrifying smiles, while a completely angular man (sharp nose, sharp chin, pointy shoulders, pointy fingers) kept lifting my hair as if aerating it would release some genie. After a few minutes, the angular man shimmied over to my mother. I did not try to understand the words or the shape their conjuration would take and when he shimmied back to my chair, he winked at me. Best to submit! To stay silent! Not to move!

For the time it took him to cut my hair, I sat with my eyes closed, impassive, in a crystal bubble, hiding my humiliation, with a shell over my skin. I could no longer feel the brush working away elsewhere, at another's head, another's hair, and the sound of scissors was harder and harder to hear, they seemed to come from far away, from another room, another building, very soon from another world. In this luxurious hairdresser's salon, I wanted to learn how to keep myself under complete control, that is, to learn to be wise enough to regard without effect or incidence the grotesque that often assails us. When I opened my eyes, I would be put to the test: with curls. The angular man had, as it were, crimped my hair instead of cutting it. He had given my hair a wave that made it look even longer. I sat as if made of marble and I remained marble when, as an impulsive finishing touch to his creation, the angular man gave me another wink and fixed a ribbon to my hair, a trinket as absurd as it was ridiculous.

On the ride home, I managed to dissemble my rage and smile at my mother who complimented me without pause, she praised my grace and the delicate lines of my face, my slender neck, my delicate hands, and my long lashes, all those traits that I had surely inherited from her and that so fascinated the men around her. Nothing she said could have soothed me. On the contrary, she stirred old hurts, sparked waves of aversion. All I could think of were the green pumps, the misfortune that brought two boys into the world before me, and ways of murdering. I thought of bones that could be sawed in two, of flesh that could be flayed. I thought of newborns who had never asked to be born. Once home, I slipped out the door and ran to Guido's, but this time with a broken heart and on the verge of tears. Guido gave a reassuring laugh when he saw me. He understood my misfortune and, pressing my head to his belly, he exclaimed: *As short as possible but with the illusion of length*!

That night, at the dinner table, my father and my brothers complimented my tonsure whereas it was now my mother's turn to adopt an impassive front. As for the ribbon, I kept it as trophy, pinned to my wall.

We look at a landscape of hills. We smell the earth's scent. The wind and the sun blend together on the crest of our ears. We are attentive to all palpitations, to grass that moves. We renounce all bad thoughts and declare the stars, the park, life and genderless voices to be sparkling, and pronounce dead the spectres haunting us and the phantoms surrounding us. Once again the fluttering of your eyelashes cheers my voice.

The Gold Coin

Naturally, the most memorable football matches did not take place in the stadium or on TV or even in the school courtyard but on the roof of a car park covered with grass and bordered by five apartment buildings, where about twenty boys agreed to meet as soon as possible to play a new round and to show off their speed and their skills, their prowess in dribbling and in pulling off feints or inventing new ones. Their eagerness was fanned by the many spectators who watched the neighbourhood kids' exploits—especially on Sundays when the weather cooperated—from their balconies, not hesitating to encourage us in various ways. Me, I lived the farthest out and envied those who had the privilege of their families' admiring cries when they scored a goal or executed some beautiful technical move. Fortunately, my skills in the sport at least earned me very coded congratulations from my teammates: pats on my shoulder, smacks on my rear end, thumbs up, brief and silent clapping as they watched me, pantomimes of approval that replaced words. The matches on the car park roof, accordingly, remained the most memorable, but the year I turned eleven was the year of the World Cup, which obliged each of us to choose a player to identify with. We constantly celebrated this other within and never had so many nationalities been represented in our two teams than during our matches that year. We had no fear of the most inconceivable situations, for example, one that required the German Franz Beckenbauer, notorious defender and pillar of the Mannschaft, to stop by any means necessary the German Gerd Müller, notorious striker and another pillar of the Mannschaft! For my part, I always had a fondness for the Dutch team, whose orange jerseys, too eye-catching, too glaring, shone in my eyes like evidence of a lucid detachment, a way of reminding everyone that it was just one more game, one more masquerade. Given that Cruyff, captain of the Dutch team, had already spawned two versions of himself running around our pitch, I went for Resenbrick, whose emaciated face, undulating silhouette, deceptively indolent gait and straightforward playing suited me.

To this well-known phenomenon of identification, was added another competitive twist, a rather obsessive one at that: we had to collect the cards for all the players on all the teams playing in the World Cup and glue them into an ad hoc album available for free from the newspaper vendors. But the cards, they were hardly free! To get a hold of them, we were ready to sacrifice our snack or *pain au chocolat* at recess. Since each of us soon had a large number of doubles, we set out to trade these cards for the missing ones under the most favourable conditions. It wasn't unusual to see three or four boys in this or that corner of the courtyard, heads lowered, huddled in a circle and haggling interminably in complex palavers worthy of the highest level trafficking, in which a card's value was never absolute but dependent on the nimbus of legend one could adorn it with. The *seller* held the packet in his hand and flipped steadily through the cards, one after the other, with a rhythmic 'Got . . . Got . . . Got . . . Got . . . Got . . .' intoned by the *acquirer* when he saw pictures he already had. But suddenly, after a certain number of images had paraded past, punctuated by the rhythmic 'Got,' you heard, like the prelude to potential excitement, a 'Haven't got,' followed by a solemn silence before the negotiations. In that 'Haven't got,' the acquirer had to be able to hide his emotion, that is, the importance he attached to the missing card and the price he'd be willing to pay to own it. Certain children, past masters of nuance, were able to negotiate, with utter nonchalance, a card they'd been coveting for a long time, acquiring it as if a vulgar double of one they already had, whereas others, too emotional, were systematically betrayed by the intonation of their voices, paying full price for the card they'd dreamt of having, but never an unfair price, since in the end it was about making others happy . . .

And yet, the beauty of these negotiations, the wiliness they required was occasionally skewed by deep pockets, an outlier who devalued our exchange by acquiring cards for shameless sums. One such spoilsport would provision himself at the newsstand I liked to frequent with one or two friends. Dropping five francs at a time for the precious packets while we never had more than forty or fifty centimes in our pockets. The boy, without arrogance or any aware-ness of the disproportion of his means, would order his packet in a flaccid voice. We were offended by such stupidity because stupidity is offensive. How could we give this fool the change he deserved? Our spirits grew bold, took on colour, put on ever-crazier schemes, ricocheted from one statement to another until we were out of breath and short of ideas. We had to admit that not one of our flights of fancy would survive the rigours of implementation. But I was determined not to give up.

On my mother's vanity table was a small box they'd brought back from India, made of Agra marble, its cover inlaid with semi-precious stones in the shape of a rose. Inside the box, as in a miniature vault, were five gold coins. Spurred by the longing to act, I snuck into my parents' room, I lifted the lid and I stole one of the gold coins. Four, five, was anyone really going to count them? . . . On the way to the bank, I looked at the obverse of the coin: a young woman in profile with braided hair and a wreath of edelweiss around her neck, behind her mountains symbolizing purity of the air and of emotions.

No image was going to change a step!

In the bank, no questions, no problems: in a few seconds, the gold coin was transformed into a one-hundred-franc note! With my two friends, we kept an eye out for the flaccid-voiced boy and walked into the newsstand just before him. Just as he was reaching for his usual five-franc coin, I brandished the bill and declared: *I want this much worth of cards*! Even the flaccid have some spirit. Seeing dozens of packets fall into our hands, the boy finally opened his eyes and an onomatopoeia of stupefaction passed over his face. What joy it was to see him so ruffled, beaten on his own terrain.

We were on cloud nine.

Wild with drunkenness!

Eight months later, after the theft had long been relegated to the margins of my memory, my mother called her three sons before her vanity table. She opened the marble box. One after the other, she placed the coins in the hollow of her hand and in a voice that countenanced no evasion, she asked: *Which of you stole a* vreneli? My brothers were indignant that anyone could suspect them and I was as indignant as they were. They kept repeating: *But, what? . . . How? . . .* And I, too, kept repeating: *But, what? . . . How? . . .* Then their faces became furious and mine turned just as furious. Finally they were filled with dismay and I felt every bit as dismayed. My mother convinced herself of our innocence and did not try to explain the disappearance. She even began to doubt the number of gold coins. On that occasion I had lied, but I didn't reproach myself for it, secretly concluding that an infinity of gratification doesn't necessarily need to be accompanied by an eternity of damnation.

For you, I would hunt whales, I'd raise caterpillars, glow-worms, I'd hop around the city three times on one leg, I'd walk on my hands while guessing your favourite words, I'd paint gravel different colours, hang garlands on chimneys, I'd climb mountains, invent syrups and sorbets, I'd fill one room with pollen, another with flower buds, and to finish I'd tell you about the beauty of shadows and the enigma of reflections in a single breath.

The Piece of Glass

Forlorn in the bowl on my dresser, the two goldfish, one male, one female, had no alternative but to swim round and round and eat the same food I fed them too often, to see my face bending over them, darkening their lives devoid of warmth. Contemplating these two goldfish sapped all desire to go outside, to take advantage of the sunshine that gives the woods a different smell or the rain that gives rocks a different taste. Contemplating the two goldfish kept me from climbing trees, from hollering on top of the rubbish pile, from spitting at tree bark, from drawing the silhouettes of condors or gazelles on the ground with a stick. Contemplating the two goldfish prevented me from leaning against the trunks of trees, then filling my belly button with a bit of crumpled moss or crushed larch needles or rubbed mushroom or an earthworm that would curl up there, nice and warm. As soon as I looked at the fish, their sadness became mine.

Even though I was told they probably wouldn't survive, that it might kill them, I had convinced myself I should pour them into a lake or a pond. What did they have to lose in risking their lifeless lives? My father gave in to my pestering. Together we headed towards a man-made lake he thought might not be too cold, him in front, driving, me in back with the bowl between my legs, watching my goldfish get shaken a bit, but they swam energetically for a change. They would soon know something other than the confines of their prison. Perhaps because of the light or a spot or the air, perhaps because of a flash or a reflection—my father never knew—the car suddenly swerved right, although the road was perfectly straight, and ran into a small wall.

The silence had weight.

It was crushing.

It prevented us from getting up, opening the door, our mouths, from fleeing anywhere at all with a scream and at a run. The silence held me at its mercy. Then a rattling sound set in, a rattling that came from my father's mouth as his head, non-human, rose slowly. Frightening tension. The accident had transformed my father into a monster, an abject creature that filled my field of vision. It was impossible to act, impossible to bring him back to himself, to me, to stop the rattle.

When his head, finally lifted, sat straight on his neck, then in a flash—a blessed, saving flash, a divine flash—my father recovered his face. We were saved. He got out of the car, opened the back door, took me in his arms, and hugged me. A kiss of recovery, an infinite kiss.

The bowl had broken on impact.

The goldfish lay under the pedals.

It was later, when taking off my pants, that I found the piece of glass that had slipped into one of my pockets. I liked to squeeze this piece of glass, to squeeze it against my palm until blood stained its transparency and reddened the lines of my hand.

I want to repaint the walls of my room the same shade of red as your lipstick and to dip my furniture in the same black as your mascara. I'd like to pour the grey of your eyeshadow over the terrace floor. And when I look at nature, it's always your face I'm searching for.

The Moustache

To celebrate one of my brothers' tenth birthday, my parents had rented a hall so that the thirty or so children invited could enjoy the party. It was the first time my mother had ever agreed to this kind of a gathering. Usually, birthdays were limited to immediate family. I'd helped my father and my brothers decorate and prepare the hall: multicoloured garlands, coloured lights, petals, paper flowers, setting up everything necessary for the various games and contests to be won. I was as excited as if it were my own birthday. The children, all older than me, were happy to be there. They left their gifts on a table set up for the purpose and asked how the afternoon would go. No one felt ignored or wanted to wiggle their fingers with boredom. Games and races followed one after the other in joy, with no cheating or tricks. I even saw one girl offer the magic ball she'd just won to a boy who had trouble hiding his disappointment. If I'd been able and if I'd known it was done, I'd have proposed a monument be erected in honour of this girl or I'd have built it with my own hands and why not out of sand or tree branches, why not for only a single hour! At an age when our souls—however pure they are when we are born—have already sniffed the fumes of corruption, no drama or nastiness arrived to cloud the pleasure children can find in playing together for an afternoon. Such a vision would have restored the faith of pessimists, at least with regard to the design of humanity. The sight of my mother in a purple dress that left her shoulders bare, pleased us all, especially me, so dazzling was her charm and so adept was she at finding and describing each person's particular qualities in her luminous voice. Who among these boys and girls would not have longed to have her as a mother? . . . I wanted to ask each and every one in order to bask even more fully in the joy their answers would have given me.

If these big kids didn't impress me as much as I'd expected, I had trouble turning my eyes away from certain of the girls for whom I felt prepared to fight and conquer the most war-like, the toughest, the most ruthless suitors or to battle monsters with three, five, even six heads. The comics I liked most, telling the story of Saint George slaying the dragon on my notebook covers, kept me from thinking that contemporary evils were of a different order or could be solved in a less chivalresque manner. Even though I was the smallest and the youngest at the party, I managed to wrest a moment of glory and win admiration by proving myself more cunning in a game of skill. I bagged a pencil case that many were looking at enviously and a kiss from my mother that none would have wanted to miss.

After the birthday cake, there was one last attraction: five party bombs we knew were filled with prizes. They were placed about the room and their fuses lit simultaneously. When the five bombs exploded—and the things they held scattered everywhere, some even hitting the ceiling before falling here and there—everyone lunged at the object of his or her desire or was content with whichever one fell nearest. With a cry of victory, we saw erasers or whistles or pencil sharpeners or masks (monkey, witch, Zorro) or 3D images being brandished as if they were valuable gifts or, better, a kind of magic wand that would open the doors of life behind which handfuls of exciting and unknown sensations awaited us. I witnessed this frenetic explosion without being able to join in, stupidly mollified, happy to think that such an afternoon should last for weeks. I felt a sense of vague and tender peace, was overcome by it, when I noticed a black mass next to my shoe, something ill-defined that I had to pick up before I realized that, despite myself, I'd inherited a fake moustache, thick as only the moustaches of the most virile and hirsute of men are, a moustache that woke me from my somnolence and that, in my delight, I rushed to stick on my upper lip and adjust with the gravity and precision of those bandits on TV who must constantly shake off tireless pursuers.

I felt enormously handsome and proud.

In for a penny, in for a pound, I was about to cross the room with my head held high so that no one would miss my transformation from a rather timid little boy into a red-blooded man when I felt a hand rip off my ephemeral finery, when I heard a voice that squeezed me like a tourniquet: *There's time enough yet for those eyesores.*

One day, you think about ways of killing. You think of the films you've seen, of the books you've read, you think of how to murder, to eliminate, and you're surprised, first by the number of ways, then by the ease of choosing the method that suits you best. No obsession in the face of death's aura points to the beyond. No fear. But in the mirror I will buy to make you happy, I won't need to look at myself as an assassin to fit with the idea of a possible murder or a possible matricide. Two seconds of distraction on a road and you're an orphan. Two unforgivable seconds that annihilate you, that kill your parents. On the low table in the square room, I laid out the objects that look like lottery prizes, a strange lottery, the lottery of life. There are two darts, the red and the green, the artificial orchids, the statue, there is a photograph of the beach with the swing, the green pumps, a box of fishhooks, the steak knife, the cup of sawdust, the ex-voto and the ribbon. There are objects I've already forgotten and those I haven't mentioned: a cigarette case, a globe, an amber necklace, an African mask, a bow and arrow, a sealed letter, a cane. I will collect all these objects and put them in a trunk I will coat with black paint. I will give it to you. You can throw it away, you can bury it, hide it, burn it. You can also take it home, to your place, where, tomorrow night and perhaps for a long time, I will join you.

You twirl your tongue over my lips. You say: *I will never be a mother.* With your tongue, you irritate the ridges of my ears. You say: *I'll leave that to unhappy women.* With the tip of your tongue you moisten the corner of my eye. You say: *With me there will be no such thing as a son's tears.* Then you kiss me. Then you undress. Then you murmur: *I have enough beauty to last until your death.*